T0272790

The Red Pirogue

The Red Pirogue

A Tale of Adventure
in the Canadian Wilds

Theodore G. Roberts

MINT EDITIONS

The Red Pirogue was first published in 1924.

This edition published by Mint Editions 2020.

ISBN 9781513220673 | E-ISBN 9781513267159

Published by Mint Editions®

 MINT
EDITIONS

minteditionbooks.com

Publishing Director: Jennifer Newens
Project Manager: Gabrielle Maudiere
Design & Production: Rachel Lopez Metzger
Typesetting: Westchester Publishing Services

Contents

I. A Queer Fish   7

II. The Drifting Fire   17

III. The Strange Behavior of Dogs and Men   26

IV. Obstructing the Law   34

V. Visitors to French River   44

VI. Hot Scent and Wet Trail   52

VII. A Trap for the Hungry   60

VIII. The Red Dogs at Work   69

IX. The Sick Man   79

X. In the Nick of Time   89

Chapter I

A Queer Fish

Young Ben O'Dell emerged from the woodshed into the dew and the dawning day with a paddle in his hand, crossed a strip of orchard, passed through a thicket of alders and choke cherries and between two great willows and descended a steep bank to a beach of sand and pebbles. Thin mist still crawled in wisps on the sliding surface of the river. Eastward, downstream, sky and hills and water were awash and afire with the pink and gold and burnished silver of the new day.

Ben was as agreeably conscious of the scents of the place and hour as of the beloved sights and sounds. He sniffed the faint fragrance of running water, the sweeter breath of clover blooms, the sharper scent of pennyroyal. He could even detect and distinguish the mild, dank odors of dew-wet willow bark, of stranded cedar blocks and of the lush-green stems of black rice and duck grass.

He crossed the beach to the gray sixteen-foot pirogue which was used for knocking about between the point and the island and for tending the salmon net. It wasn't much of a craft—just a stick of pine shaped by ax and draw knife and hollowed by ax and fire—but it saved Uncle Jim McAllister's canvas canoe much wear and tear. It was heavy and "crank," but it was tough.

Ben launched the pirogue with a long, grinding shove, stepped aboard and went sliding out across the current toward the stakes and floats of the net. The upper rim of the sun was above the horizon by now and the shine and golden glory of it dazzled his eyes.

It was now that Ben first noticed the other pirogue. He thought it was a log, but only for a moment. Shading his eyes with his hand he made out the man-cut lines and the paint-red glow. It was a pirogue sure enough and the largest one Ben had ever seen. It was fully twenty-five feet long, deep and bulky in proportion and painted red from end to end. It lay motionless on the upper side of the net, caught lengthwise against the stout stakes.

Ben, still standing, dipped his long paddle a dozen times and in a minute he was near enough to the strange pirogue to look into it. The thing which he saw there caused him to step crookedly and violently backward; and before he realized what he had done the crank little dugout had rolled with a snap and he was under water.

He came to the surface beside his own craft which had righted but was full of water and no more than just afloat. He swam it into shallow water, pushed it aground, threw his paddle ashore and then turned again to the river and the big red pirogue lying motionless against the net stakes.

"Nothing to be scared of," he said. "Don't know why I jumped like that. Fool trick!"

He kicked off his loose brogans one by one, dipped for them and threw them ashore.

The sun was up now and the light was brighter. The last shred of mist was gone from the river.

"It startled me, that was all," he said. "It would startle any man—Uncle Jim himself, even."

He waded until the swift water was halfway between his belt and his shoulders, then plunged forward and swam out and up toward the red pirogue. He hadn't far to go, but now the current was against him. He made it in a few minutes, however. He gripped a gunnel of the big dugout with both hands and hoisted himself high and looked inboard. At the same moment the occupant of the strange craft sat up and stared at him with round eyes. For a few seconds the two gazed in silence.

"Who are you?" asked the occupant of the red pirogue.

"I'm Ben O'Dell," replied the youth in the water, smiling encouragingly and brushing aside a bang of wet hair. "I live on the point when I'm not away downriver at school. I was surprised when I first saw you—so surprised that I upset and had to swim."

"Is that O'Dell's Point?" asked the other.

"Yes. You can't see the house for those big willows on the bank."

"Are you Mrs. O'Dell's boy?"

"Yes, I'm her son. I'm not so small as I look with just my head out of water. I guess I'd better climb in, if you don't mind, and paddle you ashore."

"You may climb in, if you want to—but I can paddle myself all right."

"Is she steady? Can I put all my weight on one side, or must I get in over the end?"

"She's steady as a scow."

Ben pulled himself up and scrambled in. A paddle lay aft. He took it up and stroked for the shore.

THEODORE G. ROBERTS

"It was a funny place to find you," he ventured.

"Why funny?" she asked gravely.

"Well—queer. A little girl all alone in a big pirogue and caught against the net stakes."

"I'm eleven years old. I caught the pirogue there on purpose because I thought I was getting near to O'Dell's Point and I was afraid to land in the dark."

"Do you know my mother?"

"No-o—not herself—but I have a letter of intr'duction to her."

They stepped ashore and crossed the beach side by side. Ben felt bewildered, despite his eighteen years of life and six feet of loosely jointed height. This small girl astonished and puzzled him with her gravity that verged on the tragic, her assured and superior manners, her shabby attire and her cool talk of "a letter of intr'duction." He possessed a keen sense of humor but he did not smile. Even the letter of introduction struck him as being pathetic rather than funny. He was touched by pity and curiosity and profoundly bewildered.

They climbed the steep, short bank.

"You are big," she remarked gravely as they passed between the old apple trees. "Bigger than lots of grown men. I thought you were just a little boy when I couldn't see anything but your head. You must be quite old."

"I'm eighteen; and I'm going to college this fall—if mother makes me. But I'd sooner stop home and work with Uncle Jim," he replied.

At that moment they cleared the orchard and came upon the ell and woodshed of the wide gray house and Mr. James McAllister in the door of the shed. McAllister backed and vanished in the snap of a finger.

"He is shy with strangers, but he's a brave man and a good one," said Ben.

Mrs. O'Dell appeared in the doorway just then.

"Mother, here's a little girl who came from somewhere or other in a big red pirogue," said Ben. "I found her out at the net. She has a letter for you."

Mrs. O'Dell was a tall woman of forty, slender and strong, with the blue eyes and warm brown hair of the McAllisters. She wore a cotton dress of one of the changing shades of blue of her eyes, trim and fresh. The dress was open at the throat and the sleeves were rolled up to the elbows. She stepped forward without a moment's hesitation and laid a strong hand lightly on one of the little girl's thin shoulders. She smiled and the blue of her eyes darkened and softened.

"A letter for me, dear?" she queried.

"Yes Mrs. O'Dell—from dad," replied the stranger.

"You are Richard Sherwood's little girl?"

"Yes, I'm Marion."

"And you came alone? Not all the way from French River?"

"Most of the way—alone. I—dad——"

Ben became suddenly aware of the fact that the queer little girl was crying. She was still looking steadily up into his mother's face but tears were brimming her eyes and sparkling on her cheeks and her lips were trembling. He turned away in pained confusion. For several minutes he stared fixedly at the foliage and green apples of the orchard; when he ventured to turn again he found himself alone.

Ben passed through the woodshed into the kitchen. There he found his uncle frying pancakes in a fever of distracted effort, spilling batter, scorching cakes and perspiring.

"Where are they?" he asked.

Uncle Jim motioned toward an inner door with the long knife with which he was working so hard and accomplishing so little. Ben took the knife away from him, cleared the griddle of smoking ruins and scraped it clean.

"You didn't grease it," he said. "I'll handle the pork and do the turning and you handle the batter."

This arrangement worked satisfactorily.

"Where'd you find her, Ben?" whispered McAllister.

"In a big pirogue drifted against the stakes of our net," replied the youth. "She was asleep when I first glimpsed her and I thought it was somebody dead. It gave me a start, I can tell you."

"It sure would. Well, I reckon she's as queer a fish as was ever taken in a salmon net on this river."

"It was a queer place to find her, all right. Who's Richard Sherwood, Uncle Jim? Do you know him? How did mother come to guess who she was?"

"I used to know him. All of us did for a few years, a long time ago. He was quality, the same as your pa—but he wasn't steady like your pa."

"Quality? You mean he was a gentleman?"

"That's what he'd ought to been, anyhow—but I reckon the woods up French River, and one thing and another, were too much for his gentility. Ssh! Here they come!"

Mrs. O'Dell and little Marion Sherwood entered the kitchen hand in hand. The eyes of both wore a suggestion of recent tears and hasty bathing with cold water, but both were smiling, though the little girl's smile was tremulous and uncertain.

"Jim, this is Dick Sherwood's daughter," said the woman. "You and Dick were great friends in the old days, weren't you?"

"We sure was," returned McAllister awkwardly but cordially. "He was as smart a man in the water as ever I saw. Could dive and swim like an otter. And a master hand with a gun! He could shoot birds a-flying easier'n I could hit 'em on the ground. John was a good shot, too, but he wasn't a match for your pa, little girl. I hope he keeps in good health."

"Yes, thank you," whispered Marion.

"Marion's pa has left French River for a little while on business, and Marion will make her home with us until he returns," said Mrs. O'Dell.

There was bacon for breakfast as well as buckwheat pancakes, and there were hot biscuits and strawberry preserves and cream to top off with. The elders did most of the talking. Marion sat beside Jim McAllister, on his left. Jim, having taken his cue from his sister, racked his memory for nice things to say of Richard Sherwood. He sang Sherwood's prowess in field and stream. At last, spooning his preserves with his right hand, he let his left hand rest on his knee beneath the edge of the table.

"And brave!" he said. "You couldn't scare him! I never knew any man so brave as Dick Sherwood except only John O'Dell."

Then a queer change of expression came over his face. Young Ben, who was watching his uncle from the other side of the table, noticed it instantly. The blue eyes widened; the drooping mustache twitched; the lower jaw sagged and a vivid flush ascended throat and chin and cheek beneath the tough tan of wind and sun. Ben wondered.

Breakfast over, the man and youth went outside, for there were potatoes to be hilled and turnips to be thinned.

"What was the matter with you, Uncle Jim?" inquired Ben.

"Me? When?" asked McAllister.

"Just a little while ago. Just after you said how brave Mr. Sherwood was—from that on. You looked sort of dazed and moonstruck."

"Moonstruck, hey? Well, I'll tell you, Ben, seeing as it's you. That little girl took a-holt of my hand when I said that about her pa. And she kept right on a-holding of it."

"Girls must be queer. I knew something was wrong, you looked so foolish. But if her father was such a fine man as you tried to make out at breakfast, what's the matter with him? You told me that the woods had been too much for his gentility, Uncle Jim."

"Sure it was—the woods or something; but he was smart and brave all the same when I knew him. I wasn't lying; but I'll admit I was telling all the good of him I could think up, so's to hearten the poor little girl. It worked, too."

"Do you know why he left French River? And why did he leave her to come all that way alone?"

"I'll ask Flora, first chance I get. I'm just as curious as yerself, Ben."

They were halfway to the potatoes with their earthy hoes on their shoulders when Ben halted suddenly and faced his uncle with an abashed grin.

"I forgot to tend the net," he said. "It may be full of salmon for all I know—and all the salmon full of eels by this time."

McAllister's long, lean frame jerked with laughter.

"That suits me fine, Ben," he exclaimed as soon as he could speak. "We'll go tend it now. I'd sooner be on the river this fine morning than hilling potatoes, anyhow; and maybe we'll find another grilse from French River."

Uncle Jim was impressed by the red pirogue. He had seen bigger ones but not many of them. In the days of his unsettled and adventurous youth, when he was a "white-water boy," chopping in the woods every winter and "stream-driving" logs every spring, he had once helped to shape and dig out a thirty-five-foot pirogue. But that had been close onto fifty miles farther upriver and back in the days of big pine timber.

"She's a sockdolager, all right," he said. "Didn't know there was any such pines left on French River. What's underneath the blankets, aft there?"

Ben stepped into the grounded craft, went aft and lifted the blankets, disclosing a lumpy sack tied at the neck with twine, a battered leather gun case and a bundle wrapped in a rubber ground sheet and securely tied about with rope.

"It's her dunnage!" exclaimed Uncle Jim. "Off you walked and left it laying! You're a fine feller to catch a young lady in a net, you ain't! Where was your wits, Ben?"

"I was upset, that's a sure thing," admitted the youth. "And I'm still a good deal puzzled about these Sherwoods," he added.

In the net they found four salmon, three still sound and one already fallen a prey to devouring eels. Several eels had entered the largest fish by way of the gills and mouth and what had been salmon was now more eel. The silver skin was undamaged and the eels were still inside.

With Marion Sherwood's baggage, the salmon and the skinful of eels, Ben and his uncle had to make two trips from the river to the house. The eels were thrown to the hogs as they were, alive and in their attractive container. The undamaged fish were cleaned, salted and hung in the smokehouse. During that operation and the journey to the potato field and between brisk bouts of hoe work, James McAllister told his nephew most of what he knew of the Sherwoods of French River.

Mr. Richard Sherwood first appeared at O'Dell's Point twenty-six years ago when James McAllister was only twenty years of age. He was direct from England, by way of the big town sixty miles downriver. He arrived with three loaded canoes and six Maliseet canoemen from the reservation near Kingstown and jumped knee-deep into the water before the canoes could make the shore and set up a shout that started the echoes on the far side of the river.

"Jack O'Dell. Guncotton Jack! Tally-ho! Steady the Buffs!"

The Maliseets wondered; the mowers on island and mainland ceased their labors to give ear; and John O'Dell, in the orchard, hooked his scythe into the crotch of an apple tree and started for the beach at top speed with Jim McAllister close at his heels. O'Dell went down the bank in two jumps. The stranger saw him and splashed ashore. They met halfway between the willows and the water and shook hands two-handed. They were certainly glad to see each other.

That was how Richard Sherwood came to O'Dell's Point. He was a fine-looking young man, red and brown, with a swagger in his shoulders and a laugh in his dark eyes. But all the world was young then. Even Captain John O'Dell was only twenty-six.

Sherwood had been a lieutenant in O'Dell's company of the second battalion of the Buffs. The two young men had served together in a hill war in India; and Sherwood had been present when O'Dell, refusing to accept another volunteer after three had been shot down, had advanced with a cigarette between his lips and lighted the fuse of the charge of guncotton which the first volunteer had placed under the gate of the fort. He had lighted the fuse with the coal of his cigarette, while the entire garrison shot down at him and his men shot up at the garrison and then had turned and walked downhill to the nearest cover with blood flowing down his neck, the top gone from his helmet, the guard of his sheathed sword smashed on his hip and a slug of lead in the calf of his right leg—still smoking the cigarette.

John O'Dell had resigned his commission soon after the death of his father and returned home to Canada and his widowed mother and the wide gray house at O'Dell's Point. That had been just two years before Richard Sherwood's arrival on the river.

Sherwood lived with the O'Dells until December. He was a live wire. He worked on the farm, swam in the river, shot duck and partridge and snipe, hunted moose and made a number of trips upstream in search of land to buy and settle on. He wanted thousands of acres. He had big but somewhat confused ideas of what he wanted. He liked the life. It was brisk and wild. He confided to young Jim McAllister that he wouldn't object to its being even brisker and wilder than he found it in the vicinity of O'Dell's Point. The O'Dells, he said, were just a trifle too conscious of their duty toward, and superiority to, the lesser people of the river.

Jim McAllister admired Sherwood vastly in those days and was with him on the river and in the woods as often as possible. The McAllisters lived in the next house above the point. The family consisted then of Ian and Jim and Agnes and Flora and their parents and a grandfather.

They were not like the O'Dells exactly, those McAllisters, but they were just as good in their own way. Their habitation was less than the O'Dell house by four bedrooms, a gun room, a library and a drawing-room with two fireplaces; and their farm was of one hundred and sixty acres against the square mile of mainland and forty-acre island of the O'Dells. And yet the two families were loyal friends of long standing. The first McAllister to settle on the river one hundred and ten years ago had been a sergeant in the regiment of which the first O'Dell had been the commanding officer.

Jim McAllister took Mr. Richard Sherwood upriver in December, twenty-six years ago, to introduce him to some of the mysteries of trapping fur. Sherwood was restless and traveled fast. After a time they struck French River at a point about ten miles from its mouth and within a few hundred yards of the log house of Louis Balenger. Balenger had Iroquois blood in his veins and was from the big northern province of Quebec. He had come to French River with his family five or six years before, traveling light and fast. When Jim McAllister saw where he was he urged Sherwood to keep right on, for Balenger had the reputation of being a dangerous man.

But Louis sighted them and hailed them, ran to meet them and had them within the log walls of his house as quick as winking. And there was rum on the table and the fire on the hearth burned cheerily and Mrs. Balenger said that dinner would be ready in half an hour. The dinner was plentiful and well cooked, the eyes of the Balenger girls were big and black and bright and the conversation of Louis was pure entertainment though somewhat mixed in language.

That was the beginning of Richard Sherwood's fall from grace in the eyes of the O'Dells and McAllisters and most other people of unmixed white blood on the big river. Jim McAllister returned to O'Dell's Point alone; and even he had turned his back reluctantly on the exciting hospitality of the big log house. Even as it was, he had remained under that fateful roof long enough to lose the price of a good young horse to his merry host at poker. He made all haste down the white path of French River for ten miles and then down the wider white way of the big river for twenty miles and reported to his friend John O'Dell before showing himself to his own family.

Captain O'Dell gave Jim two hours in which to rest, eat and rub the snowshoe cramps out of his legs with hot bear's grease; and then the two of them headed for French River, backtracking on Jim's trail which had scarcely had time to cool. They reached Balenger's house next day, before noon. Mrs. Balenger opened the door to them and welcomed them in. Jim McAllister followed John O'Dell reluctantly into the big living room. There sat Sherwood and Balenger at a table beside the wide hearth with cards in their hands, just as Jim had last seen them two days before.

Louis Balenger laid down his cards, sprang to his feet and advanced to meet the visitors. He expressed the honor which he felt at this neighborly attention on the part of the distinguished Captain O'Dell. But Richard Sherwood did not move. John O'Dell was very polite and cold as ice and dry as sand. He bowed gravely to Madame Balenger and her daughters, refused a glass of punch from the hand of Louis on the plea that he was already overheated and requested Dick Sherwood to settle for the play and come along. Sherwood refused to budge. He was angry and sulky.

O'Dell's Point saw nothing more of Richard Sherwood for nine long months. He appeared one August evening in a bark canoe, spent the night with the O'Dells and headed upriver again early next morning, swearing more like a river-bred "white-water boy" than an English gentleman. The captain told Jim McAllister something of what had passed between himself and Sherwood. Sherwood, it seems, had lost all his little property—the price of a good farm, at least—to Louis Balenger, and he had wanted a few hundred dollars to set about winning it all back with.

John had refused to lend him money for poker but had offered him land and stock and a home and help if he would cut his acquaintance with Louis Balenger and the entire Balenger tribe. Sherwood refused to consider any such offer, said that Delphine Balenger was worth more than all the other inhabitants of the country rolled together and that he would not lose sight of her even if he had to work his fingers to the bone in the service of Louis, and went away in a raging temper.

Once a year, for eight years, John O'Dell tried to get Sherwood away from the Balengers and French River but always in vain. Sherwood worked for Louis and according to Louis' own methods; and as he was always the goat he was frequently on the run from the wardens of the game laws.

Down at O'Dell's Point life went on evenly and honestly and yet with a fine dash of romance. Captain John O'Dell wooed and wed Flora McAllister and Jim McAllister was jilted by a girl at Hood's Ferry and several elderly people died peacefully. Up on French River, Delphine Balenger ran away with a lumberman from the States after Dick Sherwood had spent ten years in slavery and disgrace for love of her; and Sherwood set out on the lumberman's track with murder in his heart. He lost his way and was found and brought home by Delphine's younger sister. Then Sherwood quarreled with Louis Balenger and Louis shot him twice, left the Englishman for dead and vanished from French River forever. Julie Balenger nursed poor Sherwood back to life and strength and, soon after, married him.

This is what Uncle Jim told young Ben O'Dell of the Sherwoods of French River.

Chapter II

The Drifting Fire

When the little Sherwood girl first saw the library she did not believe her eyes. It was not a large room, and there were not more than six hundred volumes on the shelves; but Marion had to pull out and examine a score of the books before she believed that the rest were real. She had not known that there was so much printed paper in the whole world. She had seen only three books before this discovery of the O'Dell library, the three from which her father had taught her to read. He had told her of others and she had pictured the book wealth of the world on one shelf three feet long.

Ben O'Dell looked into the library through one of the open windows.

"Have you read 'Coral Island'?" he asked.

Marion shook her head.

"It's good," continued Ben. "But 'Treasure Island' is better. They are both on my shelves, farther along. 'Midshipman Easy' is fine, too—but perhaps it's too old for you. Have you read many books?"

"I've read three," she replied. "Dad taught me to read them. He taught Julie and me to read at the same time, and he said we were very clever. He could read as easy as anything."

"Who is Julie?" he asked.

"She is my mother," replied the little girl, with averted face. "They taught me to call her Julie when I was a baby and they used to laugh. She—she was ill two years ago—and I haven't seen her since—because she's in Heaven."

Ben's face grew red with pity and embarrassment; for a minute both were silent. He found his voice first.

"What books have you read?" he asked.

"'Rob Roy,' by Sir Walter Scott," she answered in a tremulous whisper which scarcely reached him. "It was quite a big book, in green covers—and I liked it best of all. And 'Infantry Training.' It was a little red book. Julie and I didn't find it very interesting. The third was 'The Army List.' It had dad's name in it and *your* father's too, and hundreds and hundreds of names of other officers of the king."

"But—you read those—'Infantry Training' and 'The Army List'?"

"Yes—plenty of times."

"And only one story like 'Rob Roy'?"

"We hadn't any more."

Ben O'Dell leaned his hoe against the side of the house and hoisted himself through the open window. The little girl looked at him; but, knowing that there were tears in her eyes he did not meet her glance. Instead, he took her by the hand and led her across the room to his own particular shelves of books.

"Here's what I used to read when I was your age," he said. "I read them even now, sometimes. 'Treasure Island'—you'll like that." He drew it out and laid it on the floor. "'From Powder Monkey to Admiral,' 'My Friend Smith,' 'The Lady or the Tiger,' 'Red Fox,' 'The Gold Bug,' 'The Black Arrow,' 'Robbery Under Arms,' 'Davy and the Goblin'— you'll like all these."

The little girl stared speechless at the pile of books on the floor. Ben recrossed the room, climbed through the window and reshouldered his hoe. He met Uncle Jim at the near edge of the potato patch.

"I've been waiting for you," said McAllister. "I don't want to take any advantage of you by starting in at these spuds ahead of you."

"I stopped a minute to show the little Sherwood girl some good books to read," explained the youth.

"Can she read?" asked Uncle Jim. "How would she learn to read, way up there on French River?"

"Her father taught her. He taught her and her mother to read at the same time. And her mother's dead. I'm sorry for that kid, Uncle Jim. Mighty tough, it seems to me—no mother—and to be left all alone in a big pirogue by her father. I'd like to know why he did that."

"So would I," returned McAllister. "I asked your ma and she didn't seem to know exactly. Couldn't make out anything particular from the letter nor from what the little girl told her—but it's something real serious, I guess. He had to run, anyhow. He is fond of the little girl, no doubt about it. His letter to Flora told that much. And he was mighty fond of his wife too, I reckon; and I wouldn't wonder if there wasn't more good in him than what we figured on, after all. He had wild blood in him, I guess; and Louis Balenger was sure a bad feller to get mixed up with."

They worked in silence for half an hour, hilling the potatoes side by side.

"I'd like to know why he left her in the pirogue. Why he didn't bring her all the way," said Ben, pausing and leaning on his hoe.

"How far down did he bring her?" returned McAllister.

"I don't know."

"Likely he was scared. Maybe the wardens were close onto his heels. It looks like he figgered on just coming part way with her, by his having the letter to your ma already written."

Again they fell to work and for ten minutes the hoes were busy. Then McAllister straightened his back.

"It's years since I was last on French River," he said. "I'd like fine to take another look at that country. We'd maybe learn something we don't know if we got right on the ground. We wouldn't have to be gone for long. Two days up, one day for scouting 'round and one day for the run home—four or five days would be plenty."

"When can we go?"

"Not before haying, that's a sure thing. Between haying and harvest is the best time, I reckon. I feel real curious about Dick Sherwood's affairs now—more curious than I've felt for years."

"He sounds mighty interesting to me! and I shouldn't be surprised to learn that you were wrong when you said the woods had been too much for his gentility, Uncle Jim."

"Neither would I, myself. But how d'ye figger it, Ben?"

"Well, the little girl has good manners."

"She sure has! I never saw a little girl with better manners. I'm hoping her pa hasn't done something they can jail him for—or if he has, that they can't catch 'im. I'm all for keeping the laws—even the game laws—but maybe if I'd lived on French River along with Louis Balenger instead of at O'Dell's Point alongside O'Dells all my life, I'd be busy this minute keeping a jump ahead of the wardens instead of hilling potatoes. You never can tell. There's more to shootin' a moose in close season nor the twitch of the finger. There's many an outlaw running the woods who would have been an honest farmer like yer Uncle Jim if only he'd been born a McAllister and been bred alongside the O'Dells."

"I've been thinking that myself," returned Ben gravely. "Environment, that's it! The influence of environment."

"It sure sounds right to me, all right," said McAllister. "We'll call it that, anyhow; and we won't forget that Dick Sherwood taught his little girl good manners and how to read."

The thought of getting away from the duties of the farm for a few days was a pleasant one to both the honest farmer and his big nephew.

Jim McAllister was not an enthusiastic agriculturalist. He loved the country and he didn't object to an occasional bout of strenuous toil; but the unadventurous round of milking and weeding and hoeing day after day bored him extremely even now in his forty-sixth year. But for the mild excitement of the salmon net in the river and his love for his widowed sister and his nephew and his respect for the memory of the late Captain John O'Dell he would long ago have turned his back on the implements of husbandry and taken to the woods.

Young Ben, on the other hand, was keen about farm work. He preferred it to school work. He was young enough to find excitement where none was perceptible to his uncle. He loved all growing things, but he loved cattle more than crops, horses more than cows. The practical side of farm life was dear to him and he took pleasure in the duties which seemed humdrum to his uncle; but the side issues, the sporting features, were even dearer. He loved the river better than the meadow and he saw eye to eye with McAllister in the matter of the salmon net. A flying duck set his blood flying and the reek of burned powder on the air of a frosty morning was the most delicious scent he knew. He loved wood smoke under trees and the click of an iron-shod canoe pole on pebbles, and the tracks of wild animals in mud and snow. The prospect of a visit to French River was far from unwelcome to him.

That was an unusually warm night, without a breath of air on O'Dell's Point. Ben went to bed at ten o'clock and somehow let three mosquitoes into his room with him. He undressed, extinguished his lamp and lay sweltering in his pajamas on the outside of his bed. Then the mosquitoes tuned their horns and sounded the charge. They lasted nearly half an hour; by the time they were dead Ben was wider awake than he had been at any time during the day. He went to the window and looked out at the sky of faint stars and the vague dark of the curving river. His glance was straight ahead at first, then eastward downstream.

Ben saw a light, a red light, drifting on the black river. His first thought was that it might be some one with a lantern, but in a moment he saw that the light could not be that of a lantern, for it grew and sparks began to fly from it. A torch, perhaps. The torch of a salmon spearer? Not likely! For years it had been unlawful to kill salmon or bass with the spear and there was no lawbreaker on the river possessed of sufficient hardihood to light his torch within sight of O'Dell's Point. More than this, the light was running with the current; and it was increasing every moment in height and length far beyond the dimensions of any torch.

Ben groped for his shoes and picked them up, felt his way cautiously out of the room and down the back stairs. In the woodshed he put on his shoes and equipped himself with paddle and pole. Then he ran for the river, ducking under the boughs of the old apple trees and descending the bank in a jump and a slide. Dim as the light was he saw that the big pirogue was gone before he reached the edge of the water. The sixteen-footer was there but nothing was to be seen of the giant from French River. He looked downstream and saw the light which had attracted him from his window vanishing behind the head of the island, out in the channel. It was like a floating camp fire by this time.

Ben threw pole and paddle into the sixteen-footer, ran her into the water and leaped aboard. He shot her straight across the current for a distance of several hundred yards, until he was clear of the head of the island, then swung down on the track of the drifting fire. He paddled hard, urged by a very natural curiosity. This and the disappearance of the red pirogue from the point and the fact that he was out on the dark river in his pajamas instead of tossing on his hot bed, thrilled him pleasantly.

He drew steadily down upon the fire which was now leaping high and tossing up showers of sparks and trailing blood-red reflections on the black water. As he drew yet nearer he heard the crackle of its burning and the hiss of embers in the water. He heard a dog barking off on the southern shore. He heard the roaring breath of the fire and felt its heat. He swerved slightly and drew abreast of it.

He saw that the fire was in a boat of some sort, that the vessel was full of flame and crowned with flame, that it was heaped high from bow to stern with blazing driftwood and dry brush. The lines of the craft showed black and clear-cut between the leaping red and yellow of the flames above and the sliding red of the water below. He looked more intently and recognized the lines and bulk of the big red pirogue.

The red pirogue, the property of his mother's guest, adrift and afire in the middle of the river! Who had dared to do this thing? No neighbor, that was certain. Canoes, nets, all sorts of gear, were as safe on the beach at O'Dell's Point as in the house itself. This must be the work of a stranger and of an insane one, at that.

Ben continued to drift abreast of the red pirogue and watch it burn. He kept just out of range of the showering sparks and the scorching heat. He felt indignant and puzzled. But for the assurance of his own eyes he could not have believed that any inhabitant of the valley possessed sufficient temerity thus to remove property from O'Dell land and destroy it. If he should ever discover the identity of the offender he would make him regret the action, by thunder! He would show him that the O'Dells were not all dead. No other theft of such importance as this had been made on the O'Dell front in a hundred years. But could this be properly classed as a theft? It seemed to Ben more like an act inspired by insolence than the performance of a person driven by greed or necessity.

"Hello! Hello!" hailed a voice from the gloom on the right.

"Hello," answered Ben, turning his face toward the sound.

A small sturgeon boat appeared in the circle of fierce light, paddled by a square-shouldered old man with square whiskers whom Ben recognized as Tim Hood of Hood's Ferry.

"Hold hard there!" cried Hood. "What pranks be ye up to now?"

"Pranks? What are you talking about?" returned the youth.

The old man drew alongside and peered at Ben, shading his eyes with a hand against the glare of the fire.

"Oh, it's yerself!" he exclaimed. "Well, what d'ye know about this here? What be the joke an' who be the joker?"

"That's what I'd like to know," replied Ben, turning again to contemplate the drifting fire.

The mass of wood had settled considerably by this time and was now a mound of hot crimson and orange with low flames running over it. The gunnels of the pirogue were burning swiftly, edging the long mass of glowing embers with a hedge of livelier flame. The big pirogue hissed from end to end and was girdled by misty puffs of steam.

"Looks to me like a pirogue," said old Tim Hood. "A big one, like the ones we uster make afore all the big pine was cut off hereabouts."

Ben was about to tell what he knew but he checked himself. Pride and perhaps something else prompted him to keep quiet. Why should he admit to this old ferryman that some one on the river had dared to take a pirogue from the O'Dell front? Very likely it would amuse Hood to believe that the influence of this distinguished family for honesty and order was waning, for the ferryman was the only person within ten miles of O'Dell's Point who had ever openly denied the virtue of the things for which the O'Dells of the Point had stood for more than a hundred years. During Captain John's term of occupation, and even

THEODORE G. ROBERTS

in the days of Ben's grandfather, Tim Hood had openly derided the elegant condescension of the O'Dell manners and the purity of the O'Dell speech and made light of learning, military rank and romantic traditions. So Ben did not tell the old man that the pirogue had been set adrift from O'Dell's Point.

"I saw it from my bedroom window and couldn't make out what it was," he said.

"Same here," replied Hood. "An' whatever it was, it won't be even that much longer."

He swung the sturgeon boat around and paddled away into the gloom.

Ben also deserted the fated pirogue which was now shrouded in a cloud of steam. He backed and headed his sluggish craft for the bulky darkness of the left shore.

"I'm glad I didn't tell him," he reflected. "He'd have laughed and sneered, the way he does about everything he doesn't know anything about. And I'm mighty glad I didn't say anything about the little girl— about her coming to the point all alone and me finding her drifted against the net stakes. He'd have made the worst of that—would have said Sherwood had run away and deserted her and sneered at both of them."

When he got into shallow water he headed upstream and exchanged the paddle for the pole. He had paddled and drifted far below the tail of the little island. The water was not swift and the bottom was firm. He poled easily, keeping close inshore. He searched his knowledge of his neighbors and his somewhat limited experience of life and human nature for a solution of the puzzle and for a reason for the removal and destruction of the red pirogue. But he failed to see light. The more he thought of it, the more utterly unreasonable it seemed to him. It was a mystery; and he had inherited a taste for the mysterious with his McAllister blood.

Upon reaching the tail of the island Ben kept to his course and entered the thoroughfare between the island and the left shore. Here the shallow water ran swiftly over sand and bright pebbles in a narrow passage. In some places the water was so shoal that Ben had to heave straight down on the pole to scrape over and in other places it eddied in deep pits in which water-logged driftwood lay rotting and big eels squirmed. Both the island shore and the mainland shore were grown thick and tall with willows, water maples and elms. Under the faint stars the thoroughfare was black as the inside of a hat.

Ben was almost through the dark passage, almost abreast of the head of the island, when he thrust the pole vigorously into seven feet of water instead of into seven inches and lost his balance. The crank little pirogue did the rest and Ben went into the hole with a mighty splash. He came to the surface in a second, overtook the drifting craft in a few strokes and herded it into shallow water under the wooded bank. He waded hurriedly toward the stranded bow and collided with something alive—something large and alive.

Ben was staggered, physically and in other ways, for several seconds. Then he pulled himself together, shook his O'Dell courage to the fore and jumped straight with extended arms. But the thing was gone. He stumbled, recovered his balance and listened breathlessly. Thing? It was a man! He had felt clothing and smelled tobacco. He heard a rustle at the top of the bank and instantly dashed for the sound. But the bank was steep and tangled with willows. He ripped his pajamas, he scratched his skin and finally he lost his footing and rolled back to the stranded dugout. He stepped aboard, pushed off and completed his journey.

Uncle Jim smote Ben's door with his knuckles next morning, as usual, and passed on his way down the back stairs. Ben sighed in his sleep and slept on. Mrs. O'Dell came to the door twenty minutes later and was surprised to find it still closed. She knocked and received no answer. She opened the door and looked into the little room. There was Ben sound asleep, his face a picture of health and contentment. The mother smiled with love and maternal pride.

"He is so big and young, he needs a great deal of sleep," she murmured.

Her loving glance moved from his face and she saw the front of his sleeping jacket above the edge of the sheet and her eyes widened. The breast of the jacket was ripped in three places and stained in spots and splashes with brown and green. And on one of his long arm a red scratch ran from wrist to elbow.

"Ben!" she cried.

He opened his eyes, smiled and sat up.

"Look at your arm!" she exclaimed. "And your jacket is torn! What has happened to you, Ben dear?"

Then he remembered and told her all about his midnight adventure. She sat on the edge of his bed and listened gravely. The more she heard, the graver she became.

"I bet the man I bumped into is the one who did it," concluded Ben.

"Yes—but I can't think what to make of it," she said. "Something queer is going on. Perhaps an enemy of poor Mr. Sherwood's is lurking around. I shall tell Jim, but nobody else."

"The little girl will ask about her red pirogue some day," said Ben. "It was a fine pirogue—the best I ever saw."

"We must try not to let her know that it was willfully burned," replied his mother. "The poor child has suffered quite enough without knowing that her father has an enemy mean enough to do a thing like that. We must see that no harm comes to her, Ben."

Chapter III

THE STRANGE BEHAVIOR OF DOGS AND MEN

Five days after the burning of the red pirogue, another queer thing happened at O'Dell's Point. It happened between three and five o'clock of the afternoon.

Jim McAllister had driven off downstream early that morning with two horses and a heavy wagon to buy provisions at the town of Woodstock. The round trip was an all-day job. Ben O'Dell shouldered an ax after dinner and, accompanied by the youngest of the three O'Dell dogs, went back to mend a brush fence and see if the highest hay field was ripe for the scythe. Mrs. O'Dell and little Marion Sherwood washed and dried the dinner dishes and Mrs. O'Dell took a great ham from the oven and set it to cool in the pantry. At three o'clock she and the little girl took an armful of books to the old orchard between the house and the river. Red Lily went with them; Red Chief, the oldest of the O'Dell setters, remained asleep in the kitchen.

Mrs. O'Dell and the little girl from French River returned to the house at five o'clock, having finished "Treasure Island." Red Chief arose from his slumbers and welcomed them with sweeps of his plumed tail. Mrs. O'Dell went to the pantry to see how the ham looked—and the ham wasn't there!

Some one had been in the pantry, had come and gone by way of the kitchen, and yet Red Chief had not barked. Mrs. O'Dell was not only puzzled but alarmed. A thief had visited the house of the O'Dells, a thing that had not happened for generations; and, worse still, a dog of the famous old red strain had failed in his duty. And yet Red Chief had many times proved himself as good a dog as any of his ancestors had been. Red Chief, the wise and true and fearless, had permitted a thief to enter and leave the house without so much as giving tongue. It was a puzzling and disturbing thought to the woman who held the honor of her dead husband's family so high that even the honor of the O'Dell red dogs was dear to her.

She said nothing about the stolen ham to her little guest but she took the old setter by his silken ears and gazed searchingly into his unwavering eyes. But there was neither guile nor shame in those eyes.

THEODORE G. ROBERTS

Devotion, courage, vision and entire self-satisfaction were there. The old dog's conscience was clear.

Mrs. O'Dell went through the pantry. Two loaves of bread had gone with the ham. She searched here and there through the rest of the house but could not see that anything else had been taken. Nothing of value was gone, that was certain, and she felt less insecure though as deeply puzzled. She decided not to mention the vanished food and the old dog's strange passivity to her son or her brother.

A week passed over O'Dell's Point without an unusual incident. Ben and Uncle Jim commenced haying in the early upland fields; and then O'Dell's Point received its first official visit from the law. Ben brought the horses in at noon, watered them and followed them into the cool and shadowy stable; and there he found Mel Lunt and a stranger smoking cigars. Ben was startled, for he knew Mel Lunt to be the local constable; and the consciousness of being startled drove away his natural shyness and added to his indignation at the glowing cigars. His eyes brightened and his cheeks reddened.

"Young man, what do you know about Richard Sherwood?" asked the stranger, stepping forward and knocking the ash from his cigar.

"We don't smoke in here, if you don't mind," said the overgrown youth. "It isn't safe."

"This here's Mr. Brown from Woodstock, Ben," said Lunt hastily. "He's depity sheriff of the county."

"Mel's said it. Don't you worry about the cigars, young man, but tell me what you know, an' all you know, about Richard Sherwood."

Ben's face grew redder and his throat dry.

"I must ask you—again—not to smoke—in this stable," he replied, in cracked and jerky tones.

"Yer stalling, young feller!" exclaimed the stranger. "Tell me what I'm asking you an' tell it straight. Yer trying to hide something."

Jim McAllister stepped into the stable at that moment.

"Sure he's trying to hide something, Dave Brown," said McAllister. "He's trying to hide what he thinks of you for a deputy sheriff—that you're as ignorant as you are fresh. He's remembering his manners and trying to hide your want of them. He's half O'Dell an' half McAllister; so if you two want to talk in this stable about Richard Sherwood or anything else, I guess you'd better go out first and douse those cigars in a puddle or something."

"I'm here in the name of the law, Jim McAllister," said Mr. Brown, uncertainly.

"Same here, only more so," returned Uncle Jim pleasantly.

"He's in the right of it, Mr. Brown," said Mel Lunt.

The officials left the stable, ground their cigars to extinction with the heels of their boots and came back.

"Yer darned particular," remarked the deputy sheriff.

"Nothing out of the way," returned McAllister.

"Well, we're looking for Richard Sherwood from French River," said the other. "He cleared out a couple of weeks ago an' took his little girl with him. She's gone too, anyhow. I heard he used to be a friend of the folks living here, so I come to ask if you'd seen him in the last two weeks. I didn't come to set yer darned stable afire."

"No, we haven't seen Sherwood," replied McAllister. "What's the trouble? Has he taken to poaching again?"

"It's worse than poaching, this time. I was up on French River ten days ago, taking a look over the salmon pools and one thing an' another, to see if the game wardens were onto their job, an' darn it all if I didn't trip over a bran' new grave in a little clearing. There's an old Injun who calls himself Noel Sabattis lives there, an' he told me he'd buried a dead man there a few days ago. I asked questions and he answered them; and then he helped me dig—and there was a man who'd been shot through the heart!"

"You don't say!" exclaimed McAllister. "Who was he?"

"Louis Balenger."

"Balenger? What would bring him back, I wonder? What else did you find out?"

"Nothing. We're looking for Richard Sherwood."

"What has he ever done that would lead you to suspect him of a thing like that? I used to know him and he was no more the kind to kill a man than I am. Did the old Injun say Sherwood did it?"

"No, not him. He wouldn't say a word against Sherwood. But he don't matter much, one way or the other, old Noel Sabattis! He ain't all there, I guess. He says he found Balenger in Sherwood's pirogue, dead, when Sherwood and the little girl were off trout fishing. When Sherwood come back he helped Noel dig the grave; and next day he lit out and took the girl with him—so that Injun says."

"Why don't you blame it on the Injun?"

"He didn't run away."

"That's so. Well, we haven't seen Richard Sherwood around here."

"Nor anything belonging to him, I suppose?"

Jim McAllister scratched his chin.

"We have seen his daughter," said Ben O'Dell, with dignity. "She is our guest. She's in the house now, with my mother. She's only a little girl—only eleven years old—and I hope you don't intend to question her about Balenger's death."

"That's what I heard. She's stopping here, you say, but you ain't seen her father. That's queer. How'd she come?"

Ben told of his discovery of the pirogue and the girl against the stakes of the salmon net, but he did not mention the letter which the little voyager had brought to his mother. That letter, whatever it contained, seemed to him entirely too private and purely social a matter to be handed over to the inspection of a deputy sheriff.

"Did she come down all the way from French River alone, a little girl of eleven?" asked Brown. "Is that what ye're trying to stuff into me?"

"You can't talk to Ben like that," interrupted McAllister. "He's a quiet lad but he's an O'Dell—and if you'd been born and bred on this river you'd know what I mean. Ask Lunt."

"That's right," said Lunt. "The O'Dells hev always been like that. If they tell anything, it's true—but I ain't sayin' as they always tell all that they know. Now Ben here says the girl was alone when he found her, but he ain't said that he knows she come all the way from French River alone by herself. How about that, Ben?"

"She told me that her father came part way with her," said Ben.

"How far?" asked the deputy sheriff.

"She didn't tell *me*."

"Well, maybe she'll tell *me*."

"No, she won't—because you won't ask her that or anything like it," said young O'Dell.

"What d'ye mean, I won't ask her?"

"There you go again!" interrupted Jim McAllister. "Didn't I tell you that Ben here's an O'Dell?"

"Well, what about it? I'm the deputy sheriff of this county and O'Dells are nothing to me when I'm in the performance of my duty."

"Let me try to explain," said Ben, crimson with embarrassment and the agitation of his fighting blood. "I respect the laws, Mr. Brown, and I observe them. I was taught to respect them. But I was also taught to respect other laws—kinds that you have nothing to do with—officially. Laws of hospitality—that sort of thing. My father was a good citizen—and a good soldier—and I try to do what I think he would do under the same circumstances. So if you attempt to question that—that little girl—my mother's guest—about her father—whom you're hunting for a murderer—I'll consider it my—unpleasant duty to knock the stuffing out of you!"

The deputy sheriff stared in amazement.

"Say, that would take some knocking!" he retorted. "How old are you, young feller?"

"I'm going on eighteen," replied Ben quietly.

"And you think you can best me in a fight?"

"Yes, I think I can. I'm bigger than you and longer in the reach—and I'm pretty good."

"But yer sappy. And yer all joints. I'm no giant but I'm weathered. The milk's out of my bones."

"My joints are all right, Mr. Brown. You won't find anything wrong with them if you start in questioning that little Sherwood girl about her father."

"I wasn't born on this river," said the deputy sheriff, "and I'm a peaceful citizen with a wife an' children in Woodstock, but I consider myself as good a sportsman as any O'Dell who ever waved a sword or a pitchfork. There's more man in me than deputy sheriff. I'll fight you, Ben, for I like yer crazy ideas; and if you trim me I'll go away without asking the girl a single question about her father. But if I trim you I'll question her."

Ben looked at his uncle and the lids of McAllister's left eye fluttered swiftly.

"That wouldn't be fair," said Ben, turning again to Brown. "And I can't make it fair, for I'm determined that you shall not worry my mother's guest, whatever happens. If you did manage to beat me, there'd still be Uncle Jim. So you wouldn't get a square deal."

Brown looked at McAllister.

"Does he mean that *you* would object to me asking the girl a few civil questions?" he inquired.

"Sure, I'd object," said McAllister.

"But you ain't one of these O'Dells!"

"I'm a McAllister—the same kind even if not exactly the same quality."

Mr. Brown looked puzzled.

"I'm a little above the average myself," he said thoughtfully. "Tell me why you two've got to bellyaching so about me wanting to ask that little girl a few questions, will you? Maybe I'm stupid."

"Suppose some fool of a sheriff found a dead man and thought you'd killed him and found out where you'd run to from one of your own kids," said McAllister. "The kid loves you, wouldn't hurt you for a fortune, but in her innocence she tells what the sheriff wants to know and he catches you. And we'll suppose you did it and they prove it on you. Nice game to play on your little daughter, wouldn't it be?"

The deputy sheriff turned to Mel Lunt.

"How does it strike you, Mel?" he asked.

"It's a highfalutin' notion, all right for O'Dells an' sich, but no good for ordinary folks like us," replied the constable.

"Is *that* so!" exclaimed Mr. Brown. "You guess again, blast yer cheek! If you can't see why a little girl hadn't ought to be set to catch her own father an' maybe send him to jail or worse, I can. Yes, I can see it, by thunder! Any gentleman could, once it was explained to him. So you don't have to worry about that, Ben."

At that moment a gong sounded.

"That's for dinner," said Ben, "and I know my mother will be delighted if you'll dine with us. Uncle Jim, will you take them to the house while I feed the horses?"

McAllister said a few words in his sister's ear which at once enlightened and reassured her. There were fresh salmon and green peas for dinner and custard pies. The meal was eaten in the dining room. Badly painted and sadly cracked pictures of O'Dells, male and female, wonderfully uniformed and gowned, looked out from the low walls.

The deputy sheriff rose to the portraits and the old table silver. His manners were almost too good to be true and his conversation was elegant in tone and matter. He amused Ben O'Dell and McAllister and quite dazzled little Marion Sherwood; but it was impossible to know, by looking at her, whether Mrs. O'Dell was dazzled or amused. Her attitude toward her unexpected guests left nothing to be desired. A bishop and a dean could not have expected more; two old Maliseets at her table would not have received less.

Only Mel Lunt of the whole company did not play the game. He opened his mouth only to eat. He raised his eyes from his plate only to glance swiftly from one painted and sword-girt gentleman on the wall to another and then at the brow and nose of young Ben O'Dell which were the brow and nose of the portraits; and all his thought was that a deputy sheriff was pretty small potatoes after all and that a rural constable was simply nothing and none to a hill.

A little later Mel Lunt's mare was hitched to the buggy and Mel had the reins in his hands when Mr. Brown paused suddenly with one foot on the step.

"Guess I might's well take a look at the pirogue," he said, with his face turned over his shoulder toward Ben and McAllister.

"She's gone," replied Ben. "She was taken off our beach one night nearly two weeks ago."

The deputy sheriff lowered his foot and turned around.

"Taken?" he asked. "Who took her?"

Ben said that he didn't know and explained that he believed she had been taken, because she would have run aground on the head of the island if she'd simply drifted off.

"That sounds reasonable," returned Brown. "Heard anything of her being picked up below here?"

"Not a word," said Ben.

The deputy sheriff climbed to the seat beside the constable then and the pair drove away.

Ben and Jim McAllister returned to the haying and worked in the high fields until after sundown. Little Marion Sherwood went to bed immediately after supper. Uncle Jim went next, yawning, and was soon followed by Ben. The moment Ben sank his head on his pillow he discovered that he wasn't nearly so sleepy as he had thought. For a few minutes he lay and pictured the fight between himself and the deputy sheriff which had not taken place. He was sorry it had not materialized, though he felt no bitterness toward Mr. Brown. He rather liked Mr. Brown now, in fact. But what a fine fight it would have been. The thought suggested to him the great fight in "Rodney Stone," which he tried to remember, only to find that the details had become obscure in his mind. He left his bed and went downstairs with the intention of fetching the book from the library. He was surprised to find his mother busily engaged in locking and double bolting the front door.

"What's the idea, mother?" he asked. "Why lock that old door now for the first time since it was hung on its hinges?"

She told him of the disappearance of the ham and bread.

"But wasn't one of the dogs in the house?" he asked.

"Yes, Red Chief was in the kitchen; and he didn't make a sound," she answered. "He must have mistaken the thief for a friend, for you know how he is about strangers. It has made me nervous, Ben."

"And nothing was taken except the ham and bread?"

"I haven't missed anything else."

"It can't be much of an enemy, whoever it is, to let us off as easy as that. It sounds more like a hungry friend to me."

"You are thinking of Richard Sherwood, Ben."

"Yes, mother. He might be hanging 'round and not want even us to suspect it. It's an old trick I guess, from what I've read—not going as far away as the police expect you to."

"But Red Chief doesn't know Richard Sherwood. It was Red Chief's grandfather, I think, that Mr. Sherwood used to take out when he went shooting. I believe he trained several of the red dogs to the gun. He had a wonderful way with animals."

"Do you think that any of our neighbors are hungry enough to steal from us, mother? It never happened before. They always came and asked for anything they wanted."

"I am sure it was not a neighbor. I can't understand it. I am afraid, Ben."

Ben felt no anxiety concerning their safety or that of their property but he was puzzled. He could not think of any explanation of Red Chief's behavior. He did not draw his mother's attention to the fact that any one wishing to enter the old house could still do so by any one of the many windows on the ground floor, none of which had a fastening.

They entered the library together and Mrs. O'Dell held the lamp while Ben searched along his own shelves for "Rodney Stone." He found the book but he missed several others.

"Has the little girl any books upstairs?" he asked.

"No, she puts every one back in its place before supper, always."

"I wonder if Uncle Jim has 'Charles O'Malley' and 'Vanity Fair' up in his room."

"I'm sure that he hasn't—but shall we go and see?"

They went. Uncle Jim was sound asleep. The missing books were not in his room. They searched every inhabited corner of the house but failed to find either "Charles O'Malley" or "Vanity Fair."

"They were in their places yesterday," said Ben.

"They must have been taken last night," said his mother.

"And it was Red Lily who was in the house last night; the old dog and the pup were loose outside."

"Yes."

"Well, let's go to bed, mother. Who's afraid of a burglar who steals books?"

Chapter IV

Obstructing the Law

Mrs. O'Dell ceased to worry about the mysterious thefts and the red setter's failures in duty when her son presently told her what he had heard from the deputy sheriff of the tragedy on French River. Now all her anxiety was for the little girl who had come to her so trustingly in the big pirogue, the little girl whose mother was dead and whose father was a fugitive from the police. She pitied Sherwood, too, but her mental attitude toward him was more confused than her son's.

Ben refused to believe for a moment that Dick Sherwood had shot his enemy, Louis Balenger, or any other unarmed man. His reasoning was simple almost to childishness. Balenger had evidently been shot from cover and when in no position to defend himself; and that, and the fact that Sherwood had been John O'Dell's friend for years, were proof enough for Ben that Sherwood was innocent of Louis Balenger's death.

Jim McAllister wasn't so sure, but he suspected that the old Indian, Sabattis, had put something over on Sherwood as well as on the deputy sheriff and constable. Jim had known Dick Sherwood as a good sportsman; had seen him laugh at fatigue and danger; had watched him work with young dogs and young horses, training them to the gun and the bit, gentle and understanding. Jim admitted that there was wild blood in Sherwood, but no mean blood. A man like Sherwood might be fooled by a clever rascal like Balenger into forgetting some of the social duties and niceties of his kind—yes, even to the extent of breaking a game law occasionally under pressure. But it would be dead against his nature to draw trigger on an unarmed man. Jim maintained that Sherwood had been nobody's enemy but his own. But to the question of why he had run away, if innocent, he could find no answer.

Ben had an answer—but it was so vague and obscure that he had not yet found words in which to express it.

Mrs. O'Dell did not try to weaken her son's and brother's belief in the fugitive's innocence. But her knowledge of human nature was deeper than theirs both by instinct and experience. She did not judge Sherwood in her heart, however, or voice her thought that he was

THEODORE G. ROBERTS

probably guilty. He had been guilty of lesser crimes, lesser madnesses. He had forgotten his traditions and turned his back on his old friends. He had followed his wild whims at the expense of his duty to life and in the knowledge of better things; and she suspected that such a course might, in time, lead even a gentleman to worse offenses than infringements of the game laws. But she knew that he loved his child and had loved the child's mother. And so she felt nothing for him but pity.

In the short note which little Marion had brought from her father Sherwood stated his innocence of Balenger's death far more emphatically than he wrote of his love for his daughter and her mother. And yet Flora O'Dell believed in his love for the little girl and the dead woman and was not at all sure of his innocence.

The deputy sheriff and the local constable returned to O'Dell's Point within two days of their first visit. They confronted Ben and Uncle Jim as the two farmers descended to the barn floor from the top of a load of hay.

"Look a here, young feller, why didn't you tell me all you knew about that pirogue?" demanded Mr. Brown in a nasty voice, with a nasty glint in his eyes. "You went an' made yerself out the champion man of honor an' truth teller in the world an' then you went an' lied to me!"

"What was the lie?" asked Ben.

"You said somebody stole Sherwood's pirogue."

"Took it off our front, that's what I said."

"No use arguing. The pirogue was filled up with dry wood and set afire, and you know it! And you know who set her afire! Out with it— an' save yerself from jail. I'm listening."

"Old Tim Hood has been talking to you, I suppose."

"Yes, he has."

"Then you know as much about it as I do—and maybe more. Yes, and maybe more, if you know all he knows—for he's the only person I can think of around here who'd have the cheek to take anything off our front and destroy it."

"Cheek! Come off the roof! I got yer measure now, young man; so tell me why you set that pirogue afire, and be quick about it."

"I didn't set it afire, I tell you! I saw it burning from my bedroom window and paddled down after it and took a look at it. Tim Hood came out in a sturgeon boat to take a look, too. That's all I know about it."

"Say, d'ye see any green in my eye?"

"Easy there, Dave Brown!" cautioned McAllister. "You know all Ben knows about the burning of that blasted pirogue now—and now you go asking him about yer eye. What's the sense in that? That's not the way to handle a lad like Ben."

"Cut it out, Jim McAllister! You can't put any more of that high-an'-mighty, too-good-to-sneeze O'Dell slush over on me. I fell for it once, but once was enough. O'Dell! Save it to fool Injuns with!"

Ben's face was as colorless as his shirt.

"You've done it now," said McAllister grimly.

"I reckon ye've went a mite too far, Mr. Brown," said Mel Lunt.

"Come into the next barn where there's more room," said young Ben O'Dell in a cracked voice.

"I'm not fighting to-day, I'm arresting," replied Brown.

"Arresting any one in particular?" asked Uncle Jim.

"This young man."

"What for?"

"I suspect him of burning Sherwood's pirogue with the intention of destroying evidence."

Mel Lunt shook his head. McAllister laughed. Ben stood straight and grim, waiting.

"You are a deputy sheriff, Dave Brown, but you ain't the law," said McAllister. "You don't know the law—nor you don't know this river—and somebody's been filling you up with hot air. What you need is a licking to kind of clear yer brain. After that, you can tell Judge Smith down at Woodstock all about it—and see what happens. Ben's the doctor. Will you take your treatment here or in the other barn where there's more room?"

Mr. Brown lost his temper then, turned and hurled himself at Ben. Ben sent him back with a left to the chest and a right to the ribs.

"Yer in the wrong of it, Mr. Brown," complained the constable. "I warned ye that Tim Hood was sartain to git ye in wrong."

The deputy sheriff paid no attention to Lunt but made a backward pass with his right hand. Ben jumped at the same instant. There was a brief, wrenching struggle; and then the youth leaped back and dropped an automatic pistol at his uncle's feet. McAllister placed a foot on the weapon. Again Brown rushed upon Ben and again he staggered back. There was no room for circling or side-stepping in the narrow space between the load of hay and the hay-filled bays. It had to be action front or quit.

The deputy sheriff was shaken but not hurt, for young O'Dell had spared his face. He lowered his head and charged like a ram. Ben gave ground before that unsportsmanlike onset; and, alas for Mr. Brown's nose and upper lip, he gave more than ground.

"Ye'd best quit right now," wailed Mel Lunt. "Yer gittin' all messed up an' ye ain't in yer rights an' folks'll maybe think as I was mixed up in it too."

Brown made a fourth attack and tried to obtain a wrestler's hold low down on the overgrown youth; but Ben, cool as a butter firkin in a cellar, hooked him off. Brown charged yet again, and then once more, and then sat down on the floor.

They bathed his face and held cold water for him to drink. Ben fetched sticking plaster from the house, covertly, and applied strips of it here and there to his late antagonist's damaged face.

"Never see such a hammerin' since Alec Todd fit Mike Kane up to Kane's Lake twenty year ago," said Mel Lunt, extracting crushed cigars from his superior's vest pockets. "But them two fit with feet an' everything, an' Ben here didn't use nothin' but his hands. I reckon they larn ye more'n joggofy where ye've been to school. Dang me if even his watch ain't stopped!"

The deputy sheriff and the constable drove away fifteen minutes later, the deputy sheriff sagging heavily against his companion's shoulder.

"Now they'll maybe let us get along with the haying," remarked McAllister.

"And perhaps he will get along with his own job of hunting for the man who shot Balenger, instead of wasting his time talking about that pirogue," said Ben. "How would the pirogue help him? What did he mean by speaking of it as evidence?"

"Old Tim Hood's put that crazy notion into his head, where there's plenty of room for crazy notions," replied the uncle. "Old Tim's a trouble hunter and always was—a master hand at hunting trouble for other people. And he don't like the O'Dells and never did. Yer gran'pa gave him a caning once, a regular dusting, for starving an old horse to death."

"Do you think I'll have to go to jail for fighting Brown?" asked Ben with ill-concealed anxiety. "It would be a blow to mother—but I don't see what else I could do but fight him, after the things he said."

"Now don't you worry about that," said McAllister, smiling. "Brown hasn't much sense but he's got a lot of vanity—and a little ordinary horse sense too, of course. He and Mel Lunt are busy this very minute making up as likely sounding a story as they can manage between them all about how he fell down on his face."

Nothing more was seen or heard of the deputy sheriff at O'Dell's Point. He evidently carried his investigations farther afield. No further inquiries were made concerning the fate of the big, red pirogue. Nothing more was heard of Louis Balenger or Richard Sherwood.

But more bread vanished from the pantry and again the red dogs failed to give the alarm. And the stolen books reappeared in their exact places on the library shelves.

The little girl was kept in ignorance of the suspicions against her absent father and also of the thefts of food and the mysterious borrowing of the books. The others discussed the situation frequently, but always after she had gone to bed. Ben was of the opinion that Richard Sherwood was in hiding somewhere within a few miles of the house and that it was he who had helped himself from the pantry and library. He held to this opinion in spite of the behavior of the dogs.

His mother and uncle believed otherwise. They maintained that Sherwood, innocent or guilty, would go farther than to O'Dell's Point for a place in which to hide from the police. Otherwise, why run at all? they argued. He had started well ahead of the chase, judging by what they had heard, with plenty of time to get clear out of the province. Jim believed that the food and books had been taken by an Indian. He knew several Indians in the neighborhood who could read and more who were sometimes hungry because they were too lazy to work; and they were all on friendly terms with the dogs. A sick Indian would ask for food, but a well one wouldn't for fear that a little job of work might be offered him. Haying was the last time in the year to expect one of those fellows to come around asking for anything. As for the books, an Indian who was queer enough to want to read would be queer enough to take the books on the quiet and return them on the sly. That's how James McAllister figured it out.

The last load of hay was hauled in and Ben told his mother of the contemplated trip up to French River. She replied that she was afraid to be left alone with little Marion Sherwood in a house which neither doors nor dogs seemed able to guard. Ben had not thought of this, for he felt no suggestion of violence, of any sort of menace, in the mild depredations of the mysterious visitor.

THEODORE G. ROBERTS

"I'm sorry that I'm not as brave as I used to be," said Mrs. O'Dell. "I want you to have your trip. Perhaps your Uncle Ian will sleep here while you two are away. He is sometimes very reasonable and unselfish, you know, and this may be one of the times."

Ben crossed lots to the old McAllister homestead two miles above the point, where Ian McAllister, a fifty-year-old bachelor, lived in manly discomfort and an atmosphere of argument, hard work and scorched victuals with his old friend and hired man, Archie Douglas. Both Ian and Archie were known as "characters" on the river. Both were bachelors. In their earlier years, before Ian had acquired the farm of his fathers, they had been brisk fellows, champion choppers in the woods, reckless log cuffers and jam busters on the drives, noted performers of intricate steps at barn dances and plowing frolics and foolish spenders of their wages—white-water boys of the first quality, in short.

But time and the farm had changed them for better and for worse. They never left the farm now except to go to Woodstock on business and to pay the O'Dells two brief visits every month. They worked in rain and shine. They read a few heavy theological volumes and argued over them. They played chess and the bagpipes in a spirit of grim rivalry. They did the cooking week and week about and week and week about they likewise condemned the cooking.

The McAllister hay of this year had been a heavier crop than usual and the price of beef promised to be high next Easter, so Ben O'Dell found his Uncle Ian in an obliging humor. Ian promised to sleep at the O'Dell house every night while his nephew and brother were away from home.

"It be Archie's week for the cookin'," he said, "so I reckon a decent breakfast an' human supper every day for a while won't do me no harm. But what's the matter with yer ma? What's come over her? It ain't like Flora to be scairt. What's she scairt of?"

In justice to his mother Ben had to tell Ian something of the recent strange happenings at the Point. He told of little Marion Sherwood's arrival, of her father's flight from French River and the suspicions of the deputy sheriff and of the elaborate destruction of the red pirogue, but he did not mention the thefts. He feared that Ian McAllister's attitude toward a thief, even a hungry and harmless thief, would not be as charitable as his own or his mother's or his Uncle Jim's.

"Mother's more afraid for the little girl than for herself," he said. "Coming to us like that, all alone in the pirogue, mother wouldn't have anything happen to her for the world. She doesn't want her to be frightened, even. Whatever Richard Sherwood may have done, the poor little girl is innocent."

"Well, I ain't surprised to hear that Sherwood's shot that feller Balenger," said Ian. "Sherwood's been headin' for destruction a long time now, what with one foolishness an' another—an' Balenger needed shootin'. But Sherwood hadn't ought to of done it, for all that! That's what comes of bein' wild an' keepin' it up."

"I don't believe Sherwood did it," said Ben. "He was my father's friend once and Uncle Jim says he was a good sportsman, so I don't believe he would ever be coward enough to shoot an unarmed man."

"Ye never can tell," returned Ian, wagging his head. "Louis Balenger led him a dog's life for years, so I've heard tell, an' I reckon his spirit was jist about broke by the time Louis shot a hole in him an' beat it. He lived quiet enough an' law-abidin' all the years Balenger was away, I guess; an' now it looks like Balenger had come back to French River to start some more divilment an' Sherwood had up an' shot 'im. Sure it was cowardly—but once ye break a man's spirit, no matter how brave he was once, ye make a coward of him. If he didn't do it, why did he run away?"

"That's what I can't figure out, Uncle Ian—but it seems to me a good sportsman might be broken down to some kinds of cowardice and not others. His nerves might get so's they'd fail him without his—well, without his soul turning coward—or even his heart. There's many a good horse that shies at a bit of paper on the road that has the heart to pull on a load till it drops."

"Mighty deep reasonin'," said Ian McAllister. "That's what comes of schoolin'. We'll chaw it over, me an' Archie; but whatever kind of coward Richard Sherwood may be, I'll look after yer ma an' the little girl while yer away."

Ben and Uncle Jim set out for French River next morning at an early hour in the canvas canoe. They made ten miles by noon, poling close inshore all the way. They boiled the teakettle, ate the plentiful cold luncheon with which Mrs. O'Dell had supplied them and rested for an hour and a half. Six miles farther up they came to heavy rapids around which they were forced to carry their dunnage and canoe.

"Here's where he left her and the pirogue, I wouldn't wonder," said McAllister. "Once clear of the rapids, she'd be safe to make the point. But if she was my daughter, I'd take her all the way to wherever she was going, no matter what was chasing me! He ain't the man he was when I first knew him, I guess."

"Why didn't you stick to him then?" asked Ben. "What did you all drop him for, just because he got mixed up with a bad crowd? That was no way to treat a friend."

"John kept after him eight or nine years. Once a year, year after year, yer father made the trip to French River and tried to get him to break with the Balengers and offered him land and a house down to the point."

"But what did you do? You didn't do anything, Uncle Jim."

"I was leery about visiting French River, in those days. I'd seen just enough of that outfit to guess how easy it would be to get mixed up with them. And Sherwood wasn't encouraging. All he'd do would be to cuss John out for a prig and a busybody. And it's a long way between his clearing and O'Dell's Point."

"Well, he's hiding for his life now like a wounded snipe; and I guess he wouldn't be if you hadn't been so scared about your own respectability, Uncle Jim."

McAllister scratched his chin at that but said nothing.

They reached the mouth of French River before sundown and made camp there for the night. They were early astir next morning, breakfasted before the mist was off the water and then launched into the black deep tide of the tributary stream. The fall of the banks was sheer down to and beneath the water's edge. Poling was out of the question, so the paddles were used. Ben occupied the stern of the canoe, being a few pounds heavier than his uncle and a glutton for work. Wood duck and whistlers flew up and off before their approach. A mink swam across their bows. They passed old cuttings where the stumps of giant pines were hidden by a second growth of tall young spruces and firs.

They paddled for two hours before they marked any sign of present human habitation. They saw a film of smoke then, frail blue against the dark green of the forest. Ben swung into the left bank, which was considerably lower and less abrupt here than farther down, and edged the canoe against a narrow strip of muddy shore. Here was a path, deep-worn and narrow, leading up through the tangled brush; and in the shallow water lay a few rusty tins.

They ascended the path up and over the bank and through a screen of underbrush and water birches into a little clearing. At the back of the clearing stood a small log cabin with an open door and a chimney of sticks and clay. From this chimney ascended the smoke that had attracted them. When they were halfway across the clearing a short figure appeared in the black doorway.

"Injun," said Uncle Jim over his shoulder.

The man of the clearing came a short way from his threshold and sat down on a convenient chopping block. He had a pipe in his mouth and in his right fist a fork with a piece of pork rind impaled on its prongs. Odors of frying buckwheat cakes and Black Jack tobacco drifted forward and met the visitors. The visitors halted within a few yards of the old Maliseet.

"Good morning, Noel Sabattis," said McAllister.

"Good day," returned Noel, regarding the two with expressionless and unwinking eyes.

"I'm afraid your pancakes are burning," said Ben.

The Maliseet ignored this.

"You police?" he asked.

"Not on yer life!" replied Uncle Jim. "I'm Jim McAllister and this is Ben O'Dell and we're both from O'Dell's Point down on the main river."

"Come in," said Noel, getting quickly to his feet and slipping nimbly through the doorway ahead of them.

He was stooping over the griddle on the rusty little stove when the others entered the cabin. He invited them to share his meal, but they explained that they had already breakfasted. So he broke his fast alone with amazing swiftness while they sat on the edge of his bunk and watched him. A dozen or more pancakes generously doused with molasses and three mugs of boiled tea presented no difficulties to old Noel Sabattis. When the last pancake was gone and the mug was empty for the third time, he relit his rank pipe and returned his attention to the visitors. He regarded them searchingly, first McAllister and then young Ben, for a minute or two in silence.

"Li'l girl git to yer place a'right?" he asked.

"Yes, she made it, and she's safe and well," answered Jim.

"Police git Sherwood yet? You see Sherwood, hey?"

"Not that I've heard of. And we haven't set eyes on him. But Dave Brown and Mel Lunt gave us a couple of calls. They said they'd been up here and seen you."

"Dat right," returned Noel. "You t'ink Sherwood shoot dat Balenger feller maybe?"

"I don't!" exclaimed Ben.

"I hope he didn't," said Jim. "We're his friends."

"Friends? Dat good," returned the Maliseet slowly. "Didn't know he had none nowadays 'cept old Noel Sabattis."

Chapter V

Visitors to French River

Old Noel Sabattis talked more like a Frenchman than the kind of Indian you read about. He wasn't reticent. Perhaps he had a thin strain of French blood in him, from away back, long ago forgotten. He called himself pure Maliseet. His vocabulary was limited but he made it cover the ground. Sometimes he grunted in the approved Indian manner but he could say as much with a grunt as most men can with six words. His heart was in it; and with grunts and blinks of the eye and his limited vocabulary he told Ben O'Dell and Jim McAllister all that he knew about poor Sherwood.

Noel was a lonely man. He had been a widower for close upon thirty years. His children had grown up and gone to the settlements a lifetime ago. But he had refused to go to any settlement. He had left his old trapping and hunting grounds on the Tobigue and come on to French River about ten years ago. He found Sherwood and Julie and their baby on the river in the big log house that had been Louis Balenger's. They were the only regular settlers on the stream but there was a big camp belonging to a fishing club five miles farther up.

Julie Sherwood was a fine little woman though she was Balenger's daughter, and prettier than you had any right to expect to see anywhere. Sherwood was quite a man when she was close to him; but even then Noel thought that he wasn't all he might have been. He had a weak eye—honest enough, but weak; and whenever his wife was out of his sight he was like a scared buck, ready to jump at a shadow. But he was kind and generous and Noel liked him. Julie was generous and friendly, too. They offered Noel as much room as he needed in their house and a place at their table; but Noel was an independent fellow and said that he'd have a roof of his own. He set to work at chopping out a clearing within a few hundred yards of Sherwood's clearing, and Sherwood helped him.

It wasn't long before Noel Sabattis knew a great deal about Dick Sherwood and, naturally, about the Balengers. Both the man and the woman talked to him as if they trusted him; but she was the more confiding of the two. It was she who told of Sherwood's treatment at the hands of her father and her older sister. She was bitter against both her father and her sister, but she made the bitterest accusations when her husband was not within earshot, for they would have humiliated him. And he was already too humble and she was giving all her thought and love to awakening his old self-respect in his heart.

She told Noel that her father had impoverished Sherwood years ago, when she was a child of ten or eleven, by cheating at cards, and then had tricked him into his debt and his power by further cheating—and all under the guise of friendship and good-fellowship. Her mother had told her so in a deathbed confession. Then her father had tried to make a rogue of Sherwood. He had succeeded temporarily, but with such difficulty and by means of such cruel efforts that he had made a coward of him. Yes, a coward—and that was worse than all the rest, it had seemed to Julie. She told the Maliseet that he, Richard Sherwood, who had been a soldier, had no courage now except what he got from her.

Noel used to advise them to leave French River. He put it strong, in spite of the fact that he would have been desolate if they had gone. Julie said they were planning to go to the settlements as soon as the baby was big enough to travel and Sherwood agreed with her. Noel suggested that Louis Balenger might come back and pump two more bullets into Sherwood. At that the big, broken Englishman paled under his tan but the woman didn't flinch. She said that her father would never return but that she was not afraid of him anyway.

Noel and the Sherwoods lived peacefully in their adjoining clearings year after year. Noel and Sherwood trapped fur together; but Sherwood never went very far afield. His mind and nerves went "jumpy" whenever he got more than a few miles away from his wife and child. As the years passed he seemed normal enough when with them, more nearly a sound man each year; but once out of sight of them his eyes showed fear.

Noel often tried to argue him out of his fear. When a young man and a soldier he had not been afraid of hurts or life or death, so why be a coward now, Noel argued. His old enemy Balenger was gone, so what was he afraid of? He had broken game laws and stolen furs from other men's traps and even acted as Balenger's tool once in the matter of a "rigged" game of poker down in Woodstock—but he was living as honestly now as any man and had the best wife and daughter in the province. So why continue to be ashamed and afraid? He was his own master now. He had education and strong muscles. Why didn't he go away to the settlements with Julie and the child and forget all about

French River? He owed it to himself and those two, Noel argued; and if he'd only forget Louis Balenger he'd be as good a man as he'd ever been.

Strange to say, Julie did not back Noel Sabattis as strongly as she should have in his efforts to get her husband to leave the scene of his disgrace. She, brave as a tiger in her attitude toward every known peril and ready to give her life for either her husband or child, was afraid of the unknown. She was afraid of the world of cities and men beyond the wilderness. Her parents had brought her to French River when she was scarcely more than a baby but she had fragmentary memories of streets of high houses and wet pavements shining under yellow lamps and her mother in tears and a stealthy flight. Even her father, clever and daring and wicked, had been forced to flee in fear from a city! How then would Dick Sherwood fare among men? Her fear of cities haunted her like a half-remembered nightmare.

Julie said that they would leave French River in a year or two—and always it was put off another year or two.

Julie died very suddenly of a deadly cold. She was ill for only two days. It shook old Noel Sabattis even now to think of it. Sherwood was like a man without a mind for weeks. He moved about, sometimes he ate food that was placed before him, but he seemed to be without life. He didn't understand. He couldn't believe his wife was gone. Realization of his loss came to him suddenly; and Noel had to strike him, club him, to save him from self-destruction.

Sherwood's courage was all gone after that. Without Julie he knew that he was good for nothing and afraid of everything. Because he was worthless and a coward Julie had died. A doctor could have saved her and if he had lived in the settlements she could have had a doctor.

A year passed and Noel tried to arouse Sherwood. There was still the little girl to think of. Why didn't Sherwood get out with the girl and work among men and make a home for her? What right had he to keep her in the woods on French River? But Sherwood was hopeless. He knew himself for a failure. He had failed in the woods in the best years of his life, and he knew that he would fail in the settlements. He had thought it over a thousand times. Failure outside, among strangers, would make the future terrible for the child. What could he do in towns or cities now, he who clung to an old Indian and a little girl for courage to live from day to day?

Strangers? He would not dare look a stranger in the face!

But Marion might sicken suddenly as her mother had and die for the need of a doctor! Then he would be guilty of her death, as he was

THEODORE G. ROBERTS

already guilty of Julie's death—because he was weak as water and a coward! Noel was right. He would take the girl away. He would take her downriver. He would forget the few poor shreds of pride left to him and ask the O'Dells to help her and him. He would go soon, sometime during the summer, before winter at the latest.

Then Louis Balenger came back to French River, all alone, and gave Sherwood the glad hand and Noel a cigar and little Marion a gold ring from his finger. He and Sherwood talked for hours that night after Noel had returned to his own cabin. Sherwood told Noel about it in the morning, early, while Balenger still slept. Balenger had offered Sherwood a job in a big city, a job in his own business, a partnership—and comfort and education and security for the little girl. But Sherwood knew that Balenger was lying—that there would be no security with him—that the business was trickery of some sort and that a weak and cowardly tool was required in it. And Noel, who had looked keenly into Balenger's eyes at the moment of their meeting, knew that Sherwood was right.

Sherwood took his daughter fishing up Kettle Brook and told Noel not to let Balenger know where he was. He was pitifully shaken. Noel kept away from the other clearing all morning. He went away back with his ax, hunting for bark with which to patch his canoe. He was in no hurry to see more of Balenger; but he went to face him at noon. There was no sign of the visitor in or around the house. He went to the top of the bank and saw the red pirogue grounded on the narrow lip of mud, half hidden from him by the over-hanging brush. But he saw that there was something in the pirogue. He went down the narrow path and looked closer—and there lay Louis Balenger in the pirogue, dead! He had a bullet hole in him. He had been shot through the heart.

Sherwood and the little girl came home before sundown with a fine string of trout. Noel met them at their own door, cleaned the trout, then led the father away while the daughter set to work to fry the fish for supper. He told Sherwood what had happened and Sherwood was dumbfounded. He could see that Sherwood had not done the shooting. For that matter, the distracted fellow had not taken his rifle up the brook with him.

Noel showed the body—where he had hidden it in the bushes. He took Sherwood to the pirogue and showed him faint stains in it. He had tried to wash away the stains but with only partial success.

Sherwood spoke then in a whisper, trembling all over. He said that he didn't do it but that he had planned to tell Balenger to get out that night and shoot him if he refused to go. Then he grabbed Noel by the arm and accused him of killing Balenger. His eyes were wild, but old Noel kept cool. Old Noel said that he knew nothing of the shooting, that neither of them had done the thing and that the woods were wide open. Sherwood didn't care who had pulled the trigger. It was all up with him, whoever the murderer was! His only chance was to run and run quick. Every one knew what was between him and Louis Balenger and he would be hanged for a murderer if he was caught. And what would become of Marion then?

Noel had a difficult time with Sherwood, who was mad with terror for a few minutes, but he calmed him at last sufficiently to take him back to the house. Sherwood ate his supper in a quivering silence. When the little girl kissed him he burst into tears. As soon as Marion was asleep Noel and Sherwood dug a grave and buried Balenger. Sherwood worked like a tiger. His mood had changed. He was defiant. The law would never catch him to misjudge him! Fate and the world were all against him now but he would fool them! Nothing would hurt his little daughter while he was alive—and he intended to live!

He would take Marion to the O'Dells and make his way into the States and get work where no one knew he was a failure or had ever been a coward. For he was not a coward now, by Heaven! He feared nothing but the hangman. Fate had hit him just once too often, kicked him when he was down and tried to crush his little girl. But he would outwit fate!

They returned to the cabin. Sherwood's eyes gleamed in the lamplight and his face was flushed. He wrote a note, telling Noel it was for Mrs. O'Dell, the widow of his old friend. He packed a bag, his gun and a bed roll, muttering to himself all the while. Then he went outside and looked up at the summer stars and laughed. Noel was frightened. Sherwood walked about the clearing for a few minutes, stumbling over stones and bumping against stumps and muttering like a crazy man. He quieted down and Noel got him into the house and onto his bed. He was limp as a rag by that time. Noel brewed tea for him, which he drank. He fell asleep; but he didn't get much rest, for he twitched and muttered and jumped in his sleep all night. Noel spent the night on the floor beside Sherwood's bed, wide awake.

Sherwood looked much as usual next morning, except for his eyes. There was something more than fear in his eyes, something Noel couldn't find a name for. And he wouldn't talk, beyond telling the little girl that they were going away and what she was to do with the letter which he gave her. She kissed him and asked no questions but her eyes filled with tears. Noel tried to turn him, to change his mind about running away, pointing out that if he left French River now the law would be sure that he was guilty of his enemy's death.

It was useless, even dangerous, to argue, for he turned on the old Maliseet for an instant with a look in his eyes that shook even that tough heart. Noel was wise enough to understand that misfortune had at last goaded Sherwood beyond endurance, that it was useless to reason, now that all control was gone with one who had never listened to reasoning even under the most favorable circumstances.

Sherwood put his dunnage into the pirogue. The faint stains were well forward and he covered them with ferns and stowed the dunnage over all. He placed the little girl amidships, tenderly. She was an expert canoeman but he placed her as carefully as if she were still a babe in arms. Then he paddled downstream in the big pirogue without so much as a backward glance at his friend, old Noel Sabattis.

Noel gave the pirogue a start to the first bend in the stream, then launched his old bark canoe and gave cautious chase. He was afraid of that poor, broken, weak, cowardly, crazy Dick Sherwood. Crazy, that was right! That's why he suddenly felt afraid of him.

Noel had to paddle hard to catch sight of the pirogue before it turned into the main river. He kept close inshore, glimpsing the pirogue every now and again without showing himself in return. He saw Sherwood and the child disembark at the head of the rapids and make a line fast to the stern of the big dugout and drop it slowly down through the white and black water. That eased his anxiety considerably, for he saw that Sherwood was sane in his care of little Marion, at least. Had he been mad in every respect he would have run the rapids or made a try at it.

Noel carried his canoe around to the pool below; when he next caught sight of the big pirogue he was astonished to see that the little girl was in the stern, paddling steadily and easily and that Sherwood had vanished. Perhaps Sherwood had taken to the woods in a spasm of terror or perhaps he was still in the pirogue, lying low. Noel continued to follow cautiously. He saw nothing more of Sherwood. He saw Marion rest and drift. He saw her eat. Once she ran the bow of the pirogue against the beach and remained there for more than an hour, seated motionless, save for slow turning of her head, as if she listened and watched for something or some one. At last she continued her journey and Noel followed again. He felt quite sure that Sherwood had taken to the woods. Mad!

When within five or six miles of O'Dell's Point Noel turned and headed upstream for home. He knew that there was no dangerous water between Marion and the Point and that she would reach safe landing soon after sundown. He got back to French River next day.

That was his story. It was the story he had told to the deputy sheriff and Mel Lunt, though he had not given those worthies so detailed a version of it.

"Are you the only settler on the river?" asked Ben.

"Only one left," replied Noel.

"But don't strangers come here sometimes, sportsmen and that sort of thing?"

"Yes—but the sports who fish dis river don't come dis summer. But I see one stranger. I tell Sherwood 'bout dat feller, but he don't care. He too crazy. I tell Lunt 'bout 'im too an' Lunt call me a liar."

"What about the stranger?" asked McAllister. "Suspicious-looking character was he, or what?"

"Dat right. He come onto dis clearin' one day, sudden, an' look t'rough dat door at me an' say 'Hullo, frien', you know good feller 'round here somewheres name of Louis Balenger, hey, what?' 'Nope, don't never see Balenger,' I tell dat man. 'Balenger go off dis river ten-twelve year ago an' don't come back. You his brodder, maybe, hey?' 'Brodder be tam!' dat stranger say. 'Do bizness wid him one time. Got somet'ing for him, but it don't matter. Good day.' Den he walk off quick, dat stranger, an' I don't foller him, no. He smile kinder nasty at me, wid two-t'ree gold tooth, so I t'ink maybe Noel Sabattis may's well go right on wid cookin' his little dinner. Don't see dat stranger no more."

"When was that?" asked Ben.

"When dat feller come 'round? Four-five day afore Louis Balenger come back, maybe."

"*Before* he came back? Did you tell him about it?"

"Tell Balenger? Nope. Don't tell Balenger not'ing. Don't like dat feller Balenger, me."

"And the stranger went away? He didn't wait for Balenger?"

"Dat right. Don't see 'im, anyhow. Don't see no canoe, don't smell no smoke."

"Perhaps he hid and waited for him. Perhaps he did the shooting!"

"P'r'aps. Dat what I tell Sherwood—but he don't listen. He don't care. He don't git it, Sherwood. Too scairt. Too crazy. Tell Lunt 'bout how maybe dat stranger shoot Balenger, too. Dat when he call me a liar."

Noel showed his visitors the exact spot in which the big pirogue had lain when Balenger had been found dead in it and explained its position and that of Balenger's body.

Ben took a stroll by himself, leaving his uncle and the old Maliseet smoking and yarning. He walked up and down the river along the narrow strip of shore under the bank, a few hundred yards each way, trying to picture the shooting of Louis Balenger. Then he walked up and down along the top of the bank, sometimes at the edge of the tangle of trees and brush and sometimes in it, still trying to make a picture in his mind. He busied himself in this way until supper time.

Ben took to his blankets early that night and was up with the first silver lift of dawn. He left the cabin without waking the others, hurried down to the edge of the river, got out of his shirt and trousers and moccasins almost as quickly as it can be said and plunged into the cool, dark water. He swam down with the current a short way, out in midstream, then turned and breasted the smooth, strong river. There was gold in the east now but the shadows were deep under the wooded banks. Fish rose, breaking the surface of the water into flowing circles that widened and vanished. Birds chirped in the trees. Crows cawed from high roosts. Rose tinged the silver and gold in the east and the river gleamed. Ben swam slowly, with long strokes, thrilled with the wonder of the magic of water and wood and the new day.

Ben landed on the other side of the river in a level wash of sunshine and flapped his arms and hopped about on a flat rock. In a minute his blood raced warm again and his skin glowed. He was about to plunge in again for the swim down and across to Noel's front when his attention was attracted to the bank behind and above him by a swishing and rustling in the brush.

Chapter VI

Hot Scent and Wet Trail

B en turned and looked upward. He saw dew-wet branches shaking, as if some one or something of considerable bulk was moving in the thick underbrush at the top of the bank. A red deer most likely, perhaps a moose, possibly a bear, he reflected. He felt thrilled. Moose and deer were not uncommon things in his experience but they always gave his heart a fine tingle. The thought of a bear was yet more thrilling.

The shaking of the brush continued. The movement was progressive. Whatever the animal was, it was descending the heavily screened bank directly toward the young man. Ben realized that if it was anything as tall as a full grown moose it would be showing a head, or ears at least, by this time. The disturbance of stems, branches and foliage descended to within five yards of him. Then the round black head of a big bear emerged from the green covert.

Ben knew that bears were not dangerous except under unusual conditions and that they were never more willing to attend to their own peaceful affairs and avoid unpleasant encounters than in the late summer of a good year for berries; and yet he felt embarrassingly defenseless as he regarded the round mask and pointed muzzle. One may derive a slight feeling of preparedness in emergency from even so little as the knowledge of being strongly shod for flight or kicking or the knowledge of being toughly garbed in flannel and homespun against minor scratches. But Ben wore neither flannel, leather nor homespun to support his morale. He decided that deep water would be the only place for him if the bear should take a fancy to the flat rock upon which he stood.

The bear was evidently puzzled and somewhat discouraged by Ben's appearance. It stared at him for half a minute or more and Ben returned the stare. Then it withdrew its head from view and again the alders and birches and wide-boughed young spruces shook and tossed to its passage through them. But now the disturbance receded. It moved up the steep pitch of the bank and was lost to Ben's sight in the dusk of the forest.

"There's the power of the human eye for you!" exclaimed Ben.

THEODORE G. ROBERTS

But he was wrong. The human eye had nothing to do with it. The impulse necessary for the bear's retreat was derived from bruin's own optic nerves rather than from the masterful glare of Ben's orbs. In short, that particular bear had never before encountered an undressed human being, had been puzzled for a minute to know just what species of the animal world he belonged to and had then quite naturally jumped to the shocking conclusion that some one had skinned the poor man without killing him. So the bear had turned and retired.

Instead of plunging immediately into the brown water and swimming back to Noel's front and breakfast, Ben stepped ashore. He was interested in the bear. He was curious to know just how far he had chased it with his masterful glance. Had the big berry eater only retreated to the top of the bank or had he kept right on? If he hadn't kept right on another glance would set him going again, that was a sure thing.

Ben moved cautiously, not on account of the bear but in consideration of his own skin. Wild raspberries flourished among the tough and rasping bushes and saplings and perhaps poison ivy lurked among the groundlings. So Ben moved cautiously and slowly up the bank, parting the brush before him with his hands and looking twice before every step. But despite his care he received a few scratches. When halfway up the steep slope he paused, stood straight and glanced around him over and through the tops of the tangle. He saw the bow of his uncle's canoe outthrust from its slanting bed in the bushes on Noel's front. He saw the spot, the edge of moist dark soil, where the big pirogue and its grim freight had been discovered by Noel Sabattis.

Ben continued his cautious ascent of the bank, still with curiosity concerning the bear in the front of his mind but with the mystery of Louis Balenger's death looming largely behind it. He gained the level ground at the top of the bank, still with his gaze on his feet. He was about to stand upright again and survey his surroundings when a glitter in the moss a few inches from his forward foot caught his eye.

Ben stooped lower and picked up a sliver of white metal. It was a part of a clip for keeping a fountain pen in a pocket and he instantly recognized it as such. He stooped again and examined the moss; and, a second later, he found the pen itself. He was on his knees by this time, searching the moss with eager eyes and all his fingers. And here was something more—a little pocket comb in a sheath of soft leather.

Ben forgot all about the bear and was seized by an inspiration. He turned around and lay down flat on the moss, braving prickles and scratches. He placed his chest on the very spot where he had found the broken clasp, the pen and the comb, then raised himself on his elbows and looked to his front, his right and his left. He was now in the prone position of firing, the steadiest position for straight shooting.

Ben turned his face in the direction of the tree-screened clearings downstream on the other shore. He looked through a rift between stems and trunks and foliage, clear through and away on a slant across the narrow river to the spot of moist shore against which the big pirogue had lain with the dead body of Balenger aboard. His view was unobstructed.

"Not much under three hundred yards," he said. "Pretty shooting!"

Then he discarded his imaginary rifle, marked his position by uprooting a wad of moss, gripped the broken clasp, the pen and the comb securely in his left hand and got to his feet. His blood was racing and his brain was flashing. The bear was forgotten as if it had never been.

He descended the bank with considerably less caution than he had exerted in the ascent, but with more speed, and he paid for his haste with his skin. But the price didn't bother him. He didn't notice it. He regained the flat rock, glanced down and across over the sunlit surface of the brown water, then dived. He swam swiftly, though he kept his left hand clasped tight. When he landed and opened his hand he found the water had scarcely touched the leather case of the little comb. He donned his clothes in about six motions and leaped up the path.

Ben found McAllister and the old Maliseet busy at the little rusty stove, frying bacon and pancakes as if for a prize.

"Hullo, you were up early," said Uncle Jim. "Did you catch the first worm?"

"I guess I did something like that," answered Ben breathlessly. "Look at these."

He stepped over to the table and laid the sliver of silver, the pen and the comb in a row beside one of the tin plates. He turned to old Noel Sabattis.

"Did you ever see these before?" he asked.

"Yep, sure I see 'em afore," replied Noel. "Where you git 'em dis mornin', hey? Where you been at, Ben? What else you got?"

"A fountain pen," said McAllister. "And a slick little comb in a leather case. Where've you been shopping so early, Ben?"

Ben paid no attention to his uncle. His eyes were on Noel's wrinkled face.

"Do they belong to you?" he asked.

"Nope. What you t'ink I want wid a comb, hey?"

"Were they Sherwood's?"

"Nope. Never see t'ings like dat on Sherwood. See 'em on dat stranger I tell you about."

"I thought so!" cried Ben. "I thought so! We've got him on toast! And Sherwood's clear!"

He took up the comb.

"Look at this," he said, pointing at gilt lettering stamped into the soft leather of the case. "Read it, Uncle Jim. *'Bonnard Frères, Quebec, P. Q.'* How's that for a morning's work on an empty stomach?"

Uncle Jim was bewildered.

"The stranger came from Quebec," he said. "Sure, I get that. Noel saw these things on him, and now you've found them somewheres. It proves he was here; but Noel told us that yesterday. I can't see how it proves he shot any one—Balenger nor any one else. If you'd found his rifle, now that would be something. But a fountain pen?"

"You meet him dis mornin', hey, an' rob 'im, hey?" queried Noel.

"Nothing like it!" exclaimed Ben. "I found these things in the moss at the top of the bank on the other side of the river. That's the very spot where he lay when he fired at Balenger. He broke the snap—the clasp there—when he was wriggling about for a clear shot through the brush, I guess, and the pen and the comb fell out of his pocket. He was in such a hurry to get away after he'd fired, when he saw he'd hit, that he didn't notice the pen and comb. They were pressed into the moss. I know that's what happened; and we know he came from Quebec; and Noel knows what he looks like. That's enough, I guess—enough to save Sherwood, anyhow."

"Yer figuring quite a ways ahead, Ben," said Uncle Jim.

"He shoot Balenger a'right, sure 'nough," said Noel. "But how you show dem police he do it wid one little pen an' one little comb?"

"It's simple. You'll understand about the shooting when you see the place. It's simple as a picture in a book. And for the rest of it, he must have been a friend of Balenger's before he became his enemy. Perhaps he and Balenger were partners of some sort. Then he was a bad character, like Balenger—and dangerous. He was dangerous, right enough—and a dead shot. So the police would know something about him, wouldn't they—the Quebec police? That stands to reason. Didn't he look like a bad character, Noel?"

"Yep, mighty bad. Nasty grin on him an' bad eye, too. Dat feller scare me worse nor Balenger scare me. When he look at me, den I can't look at his eye an' I look lower down an' see dat comb an' dat pen a-stickin' outer de pocket on his breast."

"There you are," said Ben to McAllister. "Very likely the Quebec police have his photograph and thumb prints; and I guess they have more brains than Mel Lunt. I'll write down Noel's description of him and all the other particulars I know, and go to Quebec and fix it."

Ben was in high spirits, gobbled his breakfast and then had to wait impatiently for the others to finish and light their pipes. The tin dishes were left unwashed, the frying pan and griddle unscoured and the three embarked in old Noel's leaky bark and went up and across the river to the flat rock. On the way Ben told of his experience with the bear, saying that but for the peculiar behavior of bruin he would not have gone ashore and climbed the bank and found the clew that was to clear Sherwood's name in the eyes of the law.

"Just chance," he said. "But for that bear, I might have hunted a week and never happened on those things."

Uncle Jim and Noel were deeply impressed by the story of the bear.

"That was more than chance," said McAllister, voicing a whisper of his old Highland blood. "I've heard of happenings like that from old Gran'pa McAllister when I was a boy. Nature won't hide murder, he used to say. I guess yer right, Ben, after all. I reckon it'll work out the way you figure it—but it sure did look kinder mixed up to me when you first told it."

They climbed the bank above the flat rock, found the spot and there each lay down in his turn, set his elbows in the correct position and looked through and over the sights of an imaginary rifle at the spot three hundred yards away where the bad heart of Louis Balenger had suddenly ceased to function.

"Dat's right," said Noel Sabattis.

"Guess we've got him, Ben," said Uncle Jim.

The visitors set out on their homeward journey within an hour of Ben's demonstration of how the shot had been fired by the owner of the fountain pen and pocket comb. But before packing their dunnage they marked the murderer's position with a peg in the ground and blazes on several young spruces and they measured the distance in paddle lengths from that point to the point where the bullet had done its work. Then they went, in spite of old Noel's protests and Uncle Jim's willingness to

THEODORE G. ROBERTS

remain until next morning. But Ben was in a fever of impatience. Now was not the time to humor Noel's love of talk or his uncle's instinctive objections to unseemly haste. Now was the time to follow the clew, to jump onto the trail and keep going, to hammer out the iron while it was hot. This was no time for talk. They had talked enough, reckoned enough, told enough and heard enough. Now was the time for action, for speed. Ben was right, and he had his way as far as McAllister and Noel Sabattis were concerned.

Ben took the stern of the fine canvas canoe and humped all his weight onto the paddle. Not only that, but he requested a little more weight from Uncle Jim in the bow; and the canoe boiled down French River like a destroyer.

It was about five o'clock in the afternoon when they approached the thrashing, flashing head of the big rapids on the main river. Uncle Jim waved his paddle toward the landing place above the first untidy rank of jumping, jostling white and black water. The imposing shout and hum of the rapids came threateningly to their ears.

"We'll run her," cried Ben.

"D'ye know the channel?" shouted McAllister, glancing back over his shoulder.

"I asked Noel. It's close along this shore. He's often run it."

"But it ain't easy at low water. We'd best land and carry around."

"You can't miss it, Noel says. And we're in a hurry. Sit tight and keep your eye skinned, Uncle Jim. Here we go!"

They went. McAllister was an old riverman and had been down these rapids many times in past years, but never before when the river was low. In high water it was a simple matter for any good canoeman to shoot Big Rapids, but in dry seasons it was only attempted by the most skilled or most daring and not always successfully. Uncle Jim was seasoned, but he got a lot of thrills in a short time at five o'clock by the sun of this particular afternoon.

As usual, it seemed to him that the jouncing, curling, black "ripples" with their fronts shot with green and amber and their tops crested with white lather, rushed up to the canoe. That is the way with strong black and white water. The canoe seemed to be stationary, trembling slightly from bow to stern as if gathering herself to spring at the last moment to meet the shock, but otherwise as motionless as if held by ropes. Up came the raging waters, up and past the jumping, squirming canoe. Big black rocks bared themselves suddenly from white veils of froth and green veils of smooth water, shouldered at the canoe, roared at her, then vanished to the rear.

Uncle Jim felt a strong impulse, an impulse of curiosity, to look back at young Ben O'Dell. But he did not obey it. He kept his half-shut eyes to the front and now made a dig with his paddle to the right and now a slash to the left. Spray flew. The canoe jounced, shivered and jumped and yet seemed to hang unprogressing amid the furious upward and backward stream of water and rock and rocky shore. Thin films of water slipped in over the gleaming gunnels and heavy lumps of water jumped aboard and flopped aboard, now from the right and now from the left. Uncle Jim received a tubful of it smash in the chest.

Uncle Jim enjoyed it, but he did not approve of it. It was too darned reckless; and he still believed that the very least that would happen to them before they reached smooth water would be the destruction of the canoe. But he wondered at Ben. He had taught Ben to handle a canoe in rough water and smooth, but never in such rough and tricky water as this. And here was the young fellow twisting and shooting and steadying her down in a manner which McAllister had never seen surpassed in his whole life on the river. His anxiety for Ben was almost topped by his pride in Ben.

And it looked as if they'd make it, by thunder! Here was the last ripple roaring up at them, baring its black teeth between white lips. And here was the slobbering black channel, shaking with bubbles and fringed with froth, and here was the canoe fair in it. The shouldering rocks sloshed past. Through!

Uncle Jim heard a sharp *crack* clear above the tumult of the rapids. He knew what had happened without looking. Ben's paddle had snapped. He shot his own paddle backward over his shoulder. But he was too late, though he could not possibly have been quicker. The canoe swerved like a maddened horse and struck the last ledge of Big Rapids with a bump and a rip. Then she spun around and rolled over and off.

Uncle Jim and Ben swam ashore from the pool below the rapids, Ben with his uncle's paddle gripped firmly in one hand.

"We were through," said Ben. "If my paddle had lasted another ten seconds we'd have made it."

McAllister grasped his hand.

"Sure thing we were through!" he cried. "Ben, I'm proud of you! I couldn't of done it, not for my life! Never saw a prettier bit of work in a nastier bit of water in all my born days!"

Ben beamed and blushed.

"It was great, wasn't it?" he returned. "But I'm sorry about the canoe, Uncle Jim. She is badly ripped, I'm afraid. There she is, still afloat. I'll go out and fetch her in."

"But what about those things—the pen and comb?" asked Uncle Jim with sudden anxiety. "Were they with the dunnage?"

"They're safe in my pocket here, sewn in and pinned in," replied Ben. "I thought something like this might possibly happen and I wasn't taking any chances."

McAllister smiled gravely and tenderly.

"I guess you were taking more chances than you knew about, lad," he said. "But it was a fine shoot, so why worry?"

Ben took off his wet coat, jumped into the pool, swam out to the wounded canoe and brought it ashore. Together they emptied her and lifted her out of the water. Her strong, smooth canvas was torn through and ripped back for a distance of two feet and five of her tough, flat ribs were cracked and telescoped.

"We had a barrel of fun, Ben, but I reckon we didn't save much time," said Uncle Jim.

They hid the canoe where she would be safe until they could return for her, and continued their journey on foot. They walked along the edge of the river, on pebbles and smooth ledges of rock, until long after sunset. Then they climbed the high bank and hunted about for a road of some sort that might lead them to a house and food. They were on the wrong side of the river to find the highroad; and after half an hour of searching they decided that they were on the wrong side of the river for finding anything. McAllister had matches in a watertight box, so they built a big fire, made beds of ferns and dry moss and fell asleep hungry but hopeful.

Chapter VII

A Trap for the Hungry

Ben O'Dell and Jim McAllister reached home soon after dinner time next day, canoeless, baggageless and empty but very well pleased with themselves. They found Mrs. O'Dell and little Marion Sherwood drying the last spoon.

Mrs. O'Dell gave the returned voyagers just one look before replacing the chicken stew on the stove to reheat and the baked pudding in the oven. Then she looked again and welcomed them affectionately.

"I hope you had a good time," she said. "We didn't expect you home so soon. Why didn't you bring your blankets and things up with you?"

"We didn't fetch them home with us," said Uncle Jim. "Left them a long ways upriver, Flora. There wasn't much to fetch back—a few old blankets and a teakettle and a mite of grub. But we had a good time. For a little while there I was having more fun than I've had in twenty years, thanks to Ben."

"I ran Big Rapids, mother," said Ben, with a mixed expression of face and voice. "I was paddling stern, you know, and we were in a hurry, and I let her go. The water was at its lowest and worst, but we got through—all but."

"Sure we got through!" exclaimed McAllister. "It was the prettiest bit of work I ever saw! We were clean through, and we'd of been home earlier, blankets an' all, if Ben's paddle hadn't bust."

"Jim McAllister! You let Ben shoot Big Rapids at low water?—that boy? What were you thinking of, Jim?"

"Let nothing, Flora! He was aft, because he's a bigger man than I am and a better one—though a mite reckless, I must say. I warned him, but not extra strong. And he did it! If there's another man on the river could do it any better, show him to me!"

"You are old enough to have more sense, Jim. And if you did it, where's your dunnage? Why did you leave it all upriver?"

"Did you run a canoe through those rapids, Ben?" asked the little Sherwood girl. "Right down those rapids between here and French River—those rapids all full of rocks and black waves and whirlpools?"

"Yes—just about," answered Ben.

"You are very strong and courageous," she said.

Ben's blush deepened and spread.

"Oh, it wasn't much. Nothing like as bad as it looks. And we didn't quite make it, anyhow. My paddle broke off clean just above the blade just before we struck smooth water—and so we struck something else instead!"

"You are very courageous. Dad wouldn't do it, even in our big pirogue. We let it through on a rope."

"And he did right," said Uncle Jim. "Yer dad showed his sense that time. I ain't blaming Ben, you understand, for I don't. It was different with Ben. He didn't have any little girl in the canoe with him, but only a tough old uncle who was seasoned to falling into white water and black before Ben here was ever born. I enjoyed it. Ben was right, sure—but Dick Sherwood was righter, Marion. He came down those rapids with you just the way any other real good father would of done it."

The little girl said nothing to that, but she went over and stood close to Uncle Jim and held his hand. Flora O'Dell grasped her son's big right hand in both of hers. Her blue eyes filmed with tears.

"Ben, you upset in Big Rapids?" she whispered faintly.

"We were clear through, mother, and upset into the pool," he said.

"I want you to be brave," she continued, her voice very low in his ear. "But I want you to remember, dear, that you are the only O'Dell on this river now—on this earth—and that life would be very terrible for me without—an O'Dell."

Ben was deeply touched. Pity and pride both pierced his young heart. Now he fully realized for the first time the wonder and beauty of his mother, of the thing that brightened and softened in her brave eyes, her love, her loneliness, her love for him. And now she called him an O'Dell; and he knew that she thought of all O'Dells as men possessed of the qualities of his heroic father. His heart glowed with pride.

"I'll remember, dear—but we were really in a hurry, mother," he answered.

For fully ten minutes he felt twenty years older than his age.

After Ben and Uncle Jim had eaten and the little girl had gone out to the orchard with a book Ben told his mother all they had learned from old Noel Sabattis and of the clew he had discovered to the identity of Balenger's murderer. He showed her the pen and comb. She felt remorse for having doubted poor Sherwood's innocence.

"Then he must be crazy—and that is almost as unfortunate," she said. "It is almost as bad for both of them."

"I don't believe he's really insane," said Ben. "He acted like it part of the time, by Noel's account, but not all the time. He was sane enough when he dropped the pirogue down the rapids on a rope instead of trying to run them. His nerves are bad and I guess he's sick. What Noel said sounded to me as if he was sick with fever—and he's afraid—afraid of all sorts of things. But I guess he'd soon be all right if he knew he was safe from the law and was decently treated. He hasn't got Balenger to worry about now. Was any more food taken while we were away, mother?"

"You still think it is Richard Sherwood who takes the food?" she asked nervously.

"I think so more than ever now, since Noel told us about him. He hadn't the nerve to go far away from his daughter."

"I wouldn't wonder if Ben's right," said McAllister.

"I hope he isn't!" exclaimed Mrs. O'Dell in a distressed voice. "A cruel thing happened last night and it was my fault. I—I told Ian about the thefts when he asked me why I was afraid to sleep without a man in the house. I didn't want him to think me just a—an unreasoning coward. And he set a trap in the bread box last night, a steel fox trap. I didn't know anything about it. I would have taken it away if I had known."

"A trap!" cried Ben, his face flushing and then swiftly paling and his eyes darkling. "A trap in this house! To hurt some one in need of bread! If he wasn't your brother I'd—I'd——"

"Same here!" muttered Uncle Jim.

"I didn't know until this morning," continued Mrs. O'Dell, glancing from her son to her brother with horrified eyes. "I found it outside, with an ax lying beside it. He had pried it open with the ax. There was blood on it. I—I went over to see Ian then—he'd gone home early—and I saw him and told him what—how I felt. I think he understood—but that won't help the—the person who was hurt."

She was on the verge of tears but Ben comforted her.

Ben and Jim McAllister spent the remainder of the afternoon in searching the woods for the poor fellow who had put his hand into the trap. Ben was sure that the person whom they sought was Sherwood and Uncle Jim agreed with him; but whoever the unfortunate thief might be, Ben felt that he was entitled to apologies and surgical aid and

THEODORE G. ROBERTS

an explanation. These things were due to the sufferer and also to the good name of O'Dell. In setting a trap to catch a hungry thief in the O'Dell house Ian McAllister had flouted a great tradition of kindness and smudged the honor of an honorable family.

The woods were wide, the ground was dry and showed no tracks, the underbrush was thick. Their search was in vain. They shouted words of encouragement a score of times, at the top of their voices, but received no reply.

The three talked late that night after the little girl had gone to bed. Ben was determined to follow up the clew which he had obtained on French River immediately and personally, to save the poor fellow who had once been his father's friend from the blundering of the law and from destruction by his own fears. And not entirely for the sake of the old friendship, perhaps. There was their guest to consider, the brave child upstairs. His mother and uncle saw the justice of his reasoning, but without enthusiasm. His mother felt uneasy for him, afraid to have him to go to a big city on such a mission. He had been away from home for months at a time during the past six or seven years, but that had been very different. He had been at school in a quiet town on the river, among people she knew. And she feared that his efforts in Sherwood's behalf would interrupt his education. She said very little of all this, however, for she knew that in this matter her son's vision was clearer and braver and less selfish than her own. Uncle Jim felt no anxiety concerning Ben, for his faith in that youth had grown mightily of late, but he wanted to know what was to become of the harvest.

It was decided that a good Indian or two should be hired to help McAllister with the harvesting of the oats, barley and buckwheat, and that Ben should go to Woodstock next day and discuss Richard Sherwood's unhappy situation with Judge Smith and return to O'Dell's Point for a night at least before going farther. Mrs. O'Dell and Uncle Jim would do everything they could to find Sherwood and reassure him. All three were convinced by now that Sherwood and the unfortunate thief were one, in spite of the fact that the red dogs had behaved as if the thief were an old and trusted friend.

Ben set out for Woodstock after an early breakfast. The long drive was uneventful. The road was in excellent condition for a road of its kind, the mare was the best of her kind on the upper river, the sun shone and the miles rolled steadily and peacefully back under the rubber tires of the light buggy.

Ben stabled the mare at the Aberdeen House stables, saw her rubbed dry and watered and fed, then sat down to his own dinner. He was well along with his meal when Deputy Sheriff Brown walked into the hotel dining room, turned around twice as a dog does before it lies down, then advanced upon Ben's table. Ben felt slightly embarrassed. He saw that Mr. Brown's face still showed something of the effects of their last meeting. The deputy sheriff held out his hand and Ben arose and took it.

"I'll eat here too, if you don't mind," said Mr. Brown.

Ben was relieved to see that, despite the faint discoloration around the other's eyes, the expression of the eyes was friendly.

"You gave me a good one, Ben," said the arm of the law, speaking between spoonfuls of soup. "I've been thinkin' it over ever since and the more I think on it the clearer I see why you did it. I was danged mad for a spell, but I ain't mad now. Yer a smart lad, Ben, if you'll excuse me for sayin' so; and jist pig-headed enough to be steady and dependable, if you don't mind me expressin' it that way."

"It is very kind of you to think so," replied Ben.

"Oh, I'm like that. No meanness in Dave Brown. If he's wrong he's willin' to admit it once he's been shown it—that's me! I guess you were right that time in yer barn, Ben. I know darn well that you acted as if right was on yer side, anyhow."

Ben looked him steadily but politely in the eye for several seconds, then leaned forward halfway across the narrow table.

"I came down to-day to tell something important to Judge Smith and perhaps to ask his advice about it, but I think I'll tell it to you instead," he said in guarded tones.

The deputy sheriff's eyes brightened and he too leaned forward.

"Something about French River?" he whispered.

"You've guessed it, Mr. Brown. Uncle Jim and I went up there and saw old Noel Sabattis and heard all he had to tell. Among other things, we heard about that stranger Noel saw once a few days before Louis Balenger showed up again."

"There was nothin' to that, Ben. The old man said he didn't see hair nor track of him after that one minute. It wasn't even a good lie. It was jist the commencement of one—an' then Noel got wise to the fact that he couldn't git it across even if he took the trouble to invent it."

Ben smiled and sat back. The waitress was at his elbow. He ordered peach pie with cream and coffee. Mr. Brown ordered apple pie with

THEODORE G. ROBERTS

cheese on the side and tea, and the waitress retired. Again Ben leaned forward.

"That wasn't a lie, and that stranger shot Balenger," he said.

"Shoot. I'm listenin'."

"He shot him from the top of the bank on the other side of the river, upstream, exactly two hundred and eighty-six yards away."

"Was yours apple or mince?" asked the waitress, suddenly reappearing with both arms full of pieces of pie and brimming cups.

The deputy sheriff turned the face of the law on her.

"Leave it an' beat it an' don't come back to-day!" he cried.

"He came from the city of Quebec," continued Ben, "and I wouldn't be surprised to learn that the police there know something about him."

Mr. Brown looked at once suspicious and impressed.

"It wouldn't surprise you much to learn anything, Ben," he said. "Have you got him tied under yer chair? Introduce me, will you?"

Ben laughed good-naturedly, produced the pen, the comb and the broken clip and told all that he knew about them, including old Noel's searching description of the stranger's appearance.

"Ben, I hand it to you," said the deputy sheriff. "I give you best—for the second time. Yer smart and yer steady—and yer lucky! What's yer next move?"

"What would you suggest, Mr. Brown?"

"Me suggest? That's polite of you, Ben, but I'd sooner listen to you. I got a high opinion of the way you work yer brains—*and* yer luck, if you don't object to me mentionin' yer luck."

"I was thinking that you might make a special constable of me or if I'm too young for that you might engage me as a private detective, and we'll go to Quebec and find out what the chief of police there knows about an acquaintance of Louis Balenger's with three gold teeth and a scar just below his right ear."

"Exactly what I was goin' to suggest!" exclaimed Mr. Brown. "Shake on it! I'll fix it—an' the sooner the quicker. What about the day after to-morrow? If you get here as early as you did to-day we can take the two-o'clock train."

Ben spent hours of the next day searching in the upland woods and the island thickets for Richard Sherwood. The incident of the trap had increased his pity for and his sense of responsibility toward the broken fugitive. Again his efforts were unsuccessful. He found nothing—no ashes of a screened fire, no makeshift shelter, no furtive shape vanishing in the underbrush. He left a message in the woods and down among the willows, repeated on half a dozen of pages torn from his notebook and impaled on twigs. Here is the message:

> You are safe and we are your friends. The trap was a mistake.
> Please come to the house.
>
> Ben O'Dell

He told his mother and Uncle Jim what he had done and they approved of it. He and Uncle Jim drove away next morning; and he and the deputy sheriff caught the two-o'clock train for Quebec.

O'Dell's Point experienced busier days than usual after Ben O'Dell's departure on the trail of the marksman from Quebec. The harvest was heavy, and Jim McAllister was the busiest man on the river. By the application of a few plugs of tobacco as advances on wages he procured the services of Sol Bear and Gabe Sacobie, two good Indians. They were good Indians, honest and well-intentioned and hardy, but they were not good farm hands. If McAllister had hired them to take him to the head of the river they would have toiled early and late, bent paddles and poles and backs, made the portages at a jog trot and grinned at fatigue. That would have been an engagement worthy of a Maliseet's serious consideration and effort. But the harvesting of oats and barley was quite a different matter. Sol and Gabe could see nothing in the laborious pursuit of the dull oats but the wages. Squaws' work, this. So Uncle Jim had to keep right at their heels and elbows to keep them going.

Jim McAllister kept the sad case of Sherwood in his mind. After the day's work and the milking and feeding, when the Maliseets were smoking by the woodshed door and his sister and little Marion were sewing and reading in the sitting room, he wandered abroad with a stable lantern. He showed his light in the high pastures, along brush fences and through the fringes of the forest. Sometimes he whistled. Sometimes he shouted the name of the man who had tried to teach him to shoot duck and snipe on the wing half a lifetime ago. He did these things five nights running but without any perceptible result. And no food had been missed since the night the trap had been set and sprung. It looked to Jim as if his brother's cruel and stupid act had driven Sherwood away, had shattered his last thread of courage, dispelled the last glimmer of his sense of self-preservation and his last ray of hope.

THEODORE G. ROBERTS

Jim McAllister believed that misfortune, grief and fear had been too much for Dick Sherwood's sanity even at the time of Balenger's death. He believed him to have been temporarily insane even then—partially and temporarily insane. His caution at Big Rapids showed that he had then possessed at least a glimmer of reasoning power and nervous control. Friendship, companionship, assurance of his own and Marion's safety might have saved him then, Jim reflected. But now Jim couldn't see any hope for him. The trap had finished what Louis Balenger's cruelty and Julie's death had begun. Sherwood had undoubtedly taken to the limitless wilderness behind O'Dell's Point, sick, hungry, wounded and crazy with fear. He was probably dead by now.

Sunday came, a day of rest from hauling oats and barley. Sol and Gabe and Gabe's squaw breakfasted in the kitchen. Mrs. O'Dell and Uncle Jim and the little Sherwood girl breakfasted in the dining room. Uncle Jim was at his third cup of coffee and already dipping into a pocket for his pipe when his sister startled him by an exclamation.

"Hark! Who's that?"

He pricked up his ears.

"It's only the Injuns talking, Flora," he said.

"No, I heard a strange voice."

The door between the kitchen and dining room opened and old Noel Sabattis entered. He closed the door behind him with a backward kick.

"How do," he said.

His shapeless hat of weather-beaten felt was on his head, a dark pipe with a rank aroma protruded from his mouth. He held a paddle in one hand and an ancient double-barreled duck gun, a muzzle loader, in the other. Marion Sherwood stared at him wide-eyed for a moment. Then she shot from her chair, flew to him and embraced him.

"Mind yerself!" he exclaimed. "Look out for dat gun!"

"Why have you come, Noel?" she cried, pulling at his belt. "Why didn't you come to see me before? Has dad come home?"

"Nope, not yet. Two-t'ree day he come. How you feel, hey?"

"I am very well, thank you," she replied, "but worried about dad—and I've missed you. Now you must take off your hat and speak to Mrs. O'Dell, who is very kind."

McAllister and the little girl relieved the old Maliseet of his gun, paddle and hat and Mrs. O'Dell brought a chair to the table for him and fetched more eggs and bacon from the kitchen.

Noel inquired about Sherwood at the first opportunity.

"He's gone, I guess," said Jim. "I'm afraid he's done for. One night when Ben and I were away, the last night we were away, a darned nasty thing happened. My brother, Ian McAllister, set a fox trap in the pantry. Whoever has been taking the food got a hand into it and had to pry himself clear of the jaws with an ax—and nothing's been taken since. It was dirty work! If Sherwood was the man, then I guess there's no chance of ever finding him—not alive, anyhow. I've hunted for him, night and day, but ain't seen track nor hair of him. He's kept right on running till he dropped, I guess. That would jist about finish him, that trap. He'd think the whole world was against him for sure."

"Yer brodder do dat, hey?" cried old Noel, angry and distressed. "You got one fool for brodder, hey? Go trappin' on de pantry for to catch dat poor hungry feller Sherwood! You better keep 'im 'way from me, Ma-callister; or maybe he don't last long!"

"He thought it was a local thief, I guess," answered Jim.

"Maybe Sherwood don't run far," said Noel. "But he lay mighty low. You hunt 'im wid dem red huntin' dogs, hey?"

"No, I didn't take the dogs in with me. They're bird dogs. They don't follow deer tracks nor man tracks. The only scent they heed is partridge and snipe and woodcock."

Noel shook his head.

"No dog ain't dat much of a fool," he said.

Chapter VIII

The Red Dogs at Work

Jim McAllister and old Noel Sabattis set out for the woods back of the point within an hour of Noel's arrival. They took uncooked food and a kettle and a frying pan in a bag, a cold lunch and a flask of brandy in their pockets, four blankets, two waterproof ground sheets, an ax and Noel's old duck gun. They took Red Chief and Red Lily, the oldest and next older of the three red dogs. They moved inland along a thin screen of alders and choke-cherries and goldenrod until they reached a point of dense second-growth spruce and fir—this to avoid attracting the attention of Sol Bear, Gabe Sacobie and Molly Sacobie. The red dogs moved obediently "to heel" until the cover of the wood was gained.

The point of woods soon widened and merged into the unpeopled forest which lay unbroken behind the river farms for scores of miles to the right and left and spread northward for scores of unbroken miles. An eighty-rod by ten-mile strip of this forest belonged to the O'Dell property. This strip of wilderness had supplied generations of O'Dells with timber and fuel and fencing without showing a scar—nothing but a few stumps here and there about the forward fringe of it and a mossy logging road meandering in green and amber shadows. Generations of O'Dells and McAllisters had shot and hunted here without leaving a mark. Maliseets had taken toll of it in bark for their canoes, maple wood for their paddles and ash wood for the frames of their snowshoes for hundreds of years; and yet to any but the expert eye it was a wilderness that had never been discovered by man.

Jim and Noel and the dogs quartered the ground as they moved gradually northward, a man and a dog to the right, a man and a dog to left, out for five hundred yards each way and in and out again, expanding and contracting tirelessly through brush and hollow. The men kept direction by the sunlight on the high treetops and touch with each other by an occasional shrill whistle. Red Chief, the oldest dog, worked with Noel, and Red Lily with Jim.

The fact that Jim did not carry a gun puzzled Red Lily, and the fact that Noel Sabattis carried a gun and did not use it puzzled Red Chief even more. Red Lily caught the scent of partridge on leaf and moss, stood to the scent until McAllister called her off or ran forward impatiently and flushed the birds. She did these things half a dozen times and the man always failed to produce a gun or show any interest in the birds. Then she decided that he wasn't looking for birds, so she hunted hares; but he recalled her from that pursuit in discouraging tones. She smelled around for something else after that. And it was the same with Red Chief. That great dog, the present head of that distinguished old family of red sportsmen gave Noel Sabattis five chances at partridge and two at cock without getting so much as an acknowledgment out of the ancient Maliseet. The fellow didn't shoot. He didn't even make a motion with the duck gun. And yet he looked to Red Chief like a man who was after something and knew exactly what it was; so Red Chief ignored the familiar scents and tried to smell out the thing Noel was looking for.

At noon the men and dogs met and sat down beside a tiny spring in a ferny hollow. McAllister made a small fire and boiled the kettle. The cold lunch was devoured by the four and the men drank tea and smoked pipes. Then the fire was trodden out and the last spark of it drenched with wet tea leaves. The search was resumed.

The sun was down and though the sky was still bright above the treetops a brown twilight filled the forest when the efforts of the searchers were at last crowned with success. The honor fell to the lot of Red Chief. Noel was about to turn and close on the center with the intention of rejoining Jim and making camp for the night when he heard the dog yelp excitedly again and again. He hurried toward the sound. He forced his way straight through tangled brush and over mossy rocks and rotting tree trunks, straight into the heart of a tree-choked hollow. The dusk was almost as deep as night in there but he saw the red dog yelping over something on the ground. He joined the dog and looked close. The thing on the ground was a man. It was Richard Sherwood, unconscious, perhaps dead.

Noel's tough old heart failed him for a moment. It seemed to turn over against his ribs and he withdrew his glance from his friend and, for a moment, put an arm over the red dog's shoulder for support. Then he laid his gun down and produced the flask from his hip. He forced a few drops of brandy between Sherwood's colorless lips. His hand shook and some of the liquor spilled and ran into the wild, gray-shot beard. He felt unnerved—far too unnerved to go on with this thing alone. He believed that Sherwood was dead; and though he was glad of the red dog's presence he wanted human companionship, too.

He moved away a few yards and discharged the right barrel of the old gun into the tops of the gloomy forest. The report thumped and thundered through the crowding, listening forest. Reserving the left barrel for a second signal, he returned to the body, raised the inert head again and forced a little more of the brandy between the cold lips. Red Chief whined and thrust his muzzle into Sherwood's face. Noel drew back a little, gathered dry twigs and moss together blindly and set a match to them. The red and yellow flames shot up. The light steadied his nerves but did not ease his heart. He fed a few sticks to the fire, moved off hurriedly and fired the second barrel of the big gun. When the echoes of the report had thumped to silence he heard the shrill, faint whistle of Jim's reply.

Noel became aware of a new note in the dog's whines and yelps. He stooped close and saw that Sherwood's eyes were open and alive.

"I've fooled you," whispered Sherwood. "I'm as good as dead—and the little girl is safe."

Then he closed his eyes. Red Chief ceased his whining, moved back a yard and lay down. Noel built up the fire.

Red Lily came leaping to the fire, followed by Jim McAllister. She yapped with delight and anxiety at sight of Sherwood, nosed his beard, flashed a red tongue at his pale forehead. Again he opened his eyes for a few seconds.

McAllister and Noel Sabattis worked over Sherwood for hours. The poor fellow was delirious, exhausted, burning with fever and suffering intense pain. They managed to get a little brandy and about a gill of water down his throat. He did not know them. He thought Louis Balenger was there.

"I've fooled you this time," he said. "Marion is safe. Safe with people you can't scare or trick. Safe from me—and safe from you. Leave her alone—or you'll get caught in a trap—and die of it—like me."

Later, he said, "You can't touch her, Balenger. Even the red dogs would kill you. They're my friends."

His right hand and arm were in a terrible state. The hand had been crushed straight across and torn by the steel teeth of the trap which Ian McAllister, in unthinking cruelty, had set in the O'Dell pantry. Hand and wrist were dark and swollen. The arm was swollen to the shoulder. Jim bathed it with warm water, then with hot water. They applied wads of hot, wet moss to the arm; but they had no bandages and nothing of which to make bandages for the wounded hand. And in their haste they had come without medicines—without quinine or iodine.

Sherwood was still alive at dawn. He even seemed to be a little stronger and in less suffering. His arm was no worse, that was certain. They gave him a little more stimulant and a few spoonfuls of condensed milk diluted in warm water. It was evident from his appearance that he had been without nourishment of any sort for days and yet he seemed unconscious of hunger. He was far too ill and weak to feel anything but the pain of his hand and arm.

Jim set out for home after breakfast, on a straight line, to fetch in bandages and quinine and to get his sister's advice as to the wisdom of using iodine. He believed that nourishment and simple remedies would revive Sherwood so that they could safely remove him to the house in the course of a day or two. Then he would get a doctor from Woodstock, Doctor Scott whom he knew, to deal with the injured hand. He believed that the inflammation of the hand and arm could be reduced in the meantime by simple treatment. He left both dogs and the gun with Noel Sabattis and the sick man.

The searchers must have covered close upon thirty miles of ground in their hunt for Sherwood but they had not gone more than eight miles straight to the northward. McAllister traveled a bee line, pausing now and then to look up at the sun from an open glade. He reached the house within two hours and twenty minutes of leaving the camp in the secluded hollow.

Back in the heart of the tree-choked hollow old Noel Sabattis bathed Sherwood's hand and arm and applied wads of steaming moss to the arm and shoulder just as Jim McAllister had done. Sherwood and the dogs slept. Noel felt sleepy, too. He had been awake through most of last night and through half of the night before and during the past two days he had exerted himself more than usual. He blinked and blinked. His eyelids wouldn't stay up. He looked at his sleeping friend and the sleeping dogs. His eyes closed and he made no effort to open them. Instead, he sank back slowly until his head and shoulders touched the soft moss.

Old Noel Sabattis slept deep and long. The moss was soft and dry. The sun climbed and warmed the still air and sifted shafts of warm light through the crowding boughs. Sherwood lay with closed eyes, motionless, muttering now and again. Red Chief arose, shook himself, hunted through the woods for a few minutes, circled the hollow, then returned to the fallen fire and sleep. The other dog awoke a little later, scouted around for ten minutes, drank at the ferny spring and returned to sleep. The hours passed. Red Chief awoke again, sniffed the still air and got purposefully to his feet. He entered and vanished into the heavy underbrush with a single bound. Red Lily awoke in a flash and flashed after him. They were both back in less than a minute. They awoke Noel Sabattis by licking his face violently. They were in too great a hurry to be particular.

Noel awoke spluttering and sat up. The big dogs jumped on him and over him a few times, then turned and disappeared in the underbrush. The old man wiped his face with the back of his hand and reached for the duck gun. He had reloaded it before breakfast. He raised the hammers, produced two copper percussion caps from a pocket of his rag of a vest, capped each nipple and lowered the hammers to half cock. Then he crawled after the dogs. He found them awaiting him impatiently at the outer edge of the hollow. They jumped about him, nosed him and made eager, choky noises deep in their throats. They moved forward slowly and steadily then, with Noel crawling after. But they did not advance far; suddenly they lay down.

Noel listened. He heard something. He set his best ear close to ground while one dog watched him with intent approval and the other gazed straight ahead. He raised himself to his knees, lifted his head cautiously and looked to his front through a screen of tall brakes. He saw two men approaching, one of whom he recognized as Mel Lunt; and though he could see only their heads and shoulders he knew that they were placing their feet for each step with the utmost care. Also, he saw that each had a rifle on his shoulder.

Noel's round eyes glinted dangerously. Man hunters, hey! Sneaks! Sneaks sneaking around to jail poor Sherwood, hunting him down by tracking his friends. He stooped for a moment and patted each dog on the head.

"Lay close," he whispered.

He stood straight, advanced two paces and halted. He brought the old gun up so that the muzzles of the two barrels were in line with the heads of the intruders and in plain sight and the butt was within a few inches of the business position in the hollow of his right shoulder.

"How do. Fine day," he said.

Old Tim Hood of Hood's Ferry and Mel Lunt the local constable stopped dead in their tracks as if they were already shot. They didn't even lower their rifles from their shoulders. Their startled brains worked just sufficiently to warn them that a move of that kind might not be safe.

For a few seconds they stared at Noel in silence. Then Tim Hood spoke in a formidable voice that matched his square-cut whiskers.

"What d'ye mean by p'intin' that there gun at us?" he asked.

"What it look like it mean?" returned Noel.

"That's all right, Tim," said Mel Lunt. "He's a friend of mine."

"T'ell ye say!" retorted Noel.

"Well, ye know me, I guess. I was up to yer place on French River. I'm the constable, don't ye mind? Me an' Sheriff Brown was up there."

"Sure t'ing, Lunt. What you want now?"

"Ye can't talk to me like that!" exclaimed Hood. "I don't take sass from no Injun nor from no danged O'Dell! Where's this here Sherwood the law be after? Take us to 'im!"

"Keep dat rifle steady, Lunt," cautioned Noel. "An' you too, old feller. I got jerks on de finger when I was little papoose an' mighty sick one time—an' maybe still got 'em, I dunno. Got hair trigger on dis old gun, anyhow."

"Don't ye be a fool, Noel Sabattis," said Lunt. "I'm a constable. I want this man Richard Sherwood, who's suspicioned of the murder of the late Louis Balenger, an' I know ye've got him somewheres 'round here. I'm talkin' to ye official now, Noel, as the arm o' the law ye might say. Drop yer gun an' lead us to him."

"Sherwood? Ain't I told you he don't shoot dat feller Balenger? He don't shoot nobody. You ask Brown. You ask Ben O'Dell. Ask anybody. Pretty near anybody tell you whole lot you don't know, Lunt!"

"'Zat so? I'll ask Mr. Brown when I see 'im, don't ye fret! I reckon we kin stand here's long as ye kin hold up that old gun; and then—but we'll show ye all about that later."

"Maybe," said Noel. "Hold 'im good long time, anyhow."

He glanced down and behind him, under his left elbow, for an instant. Red Lily still lay flat among the ferns but Red Chief was not there. He wondered at that but he did not worry. His admiration for the red dogs was great, though his acquaintance with them had been short.

In the meantime, Jim McAllister was returning on a bee line through the woods, with iodine and quinine and bandages and boric powder in his pockets and a basket containing a bottle of milk and a dozen fresh eggs in his right hand. When he was within half a mile of poor Sherwood's retreat he was met by Red Chief. The old dog leaped about him, squirmed and wriggled, ran forward and back and forward

THEODORE G. ROBERTS

again. Jim knew that he was needed for something and quickened his pace. Red Chief led him straight. Soon the dog slackened his pace and glanced back with a new expression in his eyes. It was as if he had laid a finger on his lips for caution. Jim understood and obeyed, anxious and puzzled. He stooped, looked keenly to his front and set his feet down with care.

Jim heard voices. A few seconds later, he glimpsed the shoulders of two men among the brown boles of the forest, topping the underbrush. He saw rifles slanted on their shoulders. He set the basket of eggs and milk securely in a ferny nook and continued to advance with increased caution. He recognized the voice of Mel Lunt. Then he heard Noel's voice. He heard the old Maliseet say, "I kin hold her annoder hour yet. Den maybe git so tired me finger jerk, hey? Maybe. Dunno."

He saw Noel facing the others, standing with his back square to the dense growth of Sherwood's retreat. He saw the duck gun. In a flash he understood it all; and in another flash of time indignation flared up in him like white fire. Lunt, that brainless sneak! And old Tim Hood, whose only pleasure was derived from the troubles of others! So they had spied on him, had they? Tracked him on his errand of mercy!

McAllister ran forward. Noel saw him coming, grinned and steadied the big gun. McAllister seized a rifle with each hand and yanked them both backward over their owners' shoulders. He moved swiftly around and confronted the intruders. The glare of his gray eyes was hard and hot. He tossed one rifle behind him and held the other in readiness after a jerk on the bolt and a glance at the breech.

"Guess I go bile de kittle now," said Noel Sabattis; and he lowered the duck gun and retired. His old arms trembled with fatigue, but his old heart was high and strong.

"What have you two got to say for yerselves?" asked McAllister, turning his unnerving gaze from Lunt to Hood and back to Lunt. "Ain't you read the game laws for this year? Hunting season opens October first, as usual. Or maybe you forgot I'm a game warden."

"Cut it out, Jim McAllister!" retorted Lunt. "I'm a constable. Ye ain't forgot that, I guess."

"Sure, I know that. And as you won't be one much longer, I'll use you now. Arrest Tim Hood an' take him down to Woodstock to the sheriff—an' hand yerself over too while ye're about it. The charge is carrying loaded rifles in these woods in close season."

"None o' that," said old Tim Hood. "Ye can't fool me, Jim. Me an' Mel ain't here to kill moose or deer—an' well ye know it. We be here to take a man the law wants for murder. So back out an' set down, Mr. Jim McAllister. This ain't no job for a game warden."

"I'll be as easy on you as I can," returned Jim. "Ye're out for Sherwood, I know. Well, Sherwood didn't murder anybody. The shooting was done by a stranger from Quebec and Dave Brown and young Ben O'Dell are looking for him now in Quebec."

"I ain't been officially notified o' that," said Lunt. "As a private citizen I reckon it's a lie—an' as an officer of the law I couldn't believe it anyhow. I'm here to do my duty."

"Did you call me a liar, Mel?"

"I ain't here to pick over my words with you nor no man. I'm here to do my duty."

"Toting a rifle in close season. Show me yer warrant for Richard Sherwood's arrest."

"Show nothin'," snarled old Tim Hood.

Jim moved backward until he reached the discarded rifle. He laid the second rifle beside it. Red Lily had joined him and Red Chief at the moment of their arrival on the scene.

"Guard 'em, pups," he said.

The big red dogs stood across the rifles. McAllister walked close up to the intruders, unarmed, his hands hanging by his sides.

"Hood, ye're an old man and a spiteful one, and because of yer age I'm only telling you to get off O'Dell land as quick as you know how," he said. "I'll keep yer rifle till you pay yer fine for carrying it in close season. Beat it! But ye're not too old to kick, Mel Lunt. Ye're my own age and heft and it ain't my fault ye're not as good a man. You had ought to thought of that before you called me a liar."

He swung his right hand, wide open, and delivered a resounding smack on the constable's left ear. Lunt staggered, cursing. Jim stepped in and placed a smart left on the nose and upper lip. Lunt made a furious but blind onslaught and was met by a thump on the chest that shook his hat from his head and his socks down about his ankles. Jim was unskilled as a boxer; but he was powerful and in good condition; the Highland blood of the McAllisters and the pride of the O'Dells were raging in him and he had picked up a few notions from young Ben. He biffed Mel again, but not in a vital spot.

Old Tim Hood, that bitter soul, was not idle. He dashed toward the rifles on the ground, his square-cut white whiskers fairly bristling with rage. Murder was in his heart—but there was no courage back of it. He beheld the masks of the red dogs—wrinkled noses, curled lips, white fangs and blazing eyes. His dash stopped suddenly within a yard of the rifles. He heard throaty gurgles. The bristles went out of his whiskers. He turned and jumped away in a cold panic. But rage still shook in his heart. He stooped and fumbled in the moss and ferns for a stone with which to smash Jim McAllister on the back of the head. It was a style of attack with which he had been familiar in his younger days. He found the thing he wanted, conveniently shaped for the hand and about seven pounds in weight.

Hood straightened himself, stone in hand, just in time to glimpse a red flash. Then something struck him all over and down he went, flat on his back, and the stone went rolling. For half a second he kept his eyes open. Half a second was long enough. He saw white fangs within an inch of his face, crimson gums, a black throat, eyes of green fire. His heart felt as if it would explode with terror. He screamed as he waited for the glistening fangs to crunch into his face. He waited and waited.

Mel Lunt was glad to run as soon as he realized that McAllister was too good for him. He saw that the thing to do was to run while he could and get to Woodstock as soon as possible and interview the high sheriff of the county. There might be something in the story about the man from Quebec, though he doubted it. He needed a warrant for Sherwood's arrest, anyway; and after that he would settle with McAllister and old Noel Sabattis. So he staggered southward; and Jim sped him with a kick.

Then Jim turned and whistled Red Chief off Tim Hood's chest. The old dog came trotting, waving his red plume. Red Lily continued to stand guard over the rifles. Jim walked over to where Hood lay motionless with closed eyes.

"Get up," he said. "You ain't hurt. No one touched you."

Mr. Hood opened his eyes, sat up and looked around him.

"Lunt has gone south," said Jim. "I reckon you can overhaul him if you hurry. Beat it!"

The bitter old ferryman got to his feet without a word and headed south at a very creditable rate of speed.

IN THE CITY OF QUEBEC, in the midst of excitements and novelties, Deputy Sheriff Brown and young Ben O'Dell went earnestly and successfully about their business. Mr. Brown's mind and heart were set on catching a murderer; Ben's thoughts and efforts were all bent upon clearing and saving the innocent. The success of either meant the success of both, so they worked in perfect accord.

Ben was the superior in imagination and intelligence but Brown knew the ways of the police and of cities. Brown obtained audience with the chief of police and Ben's manner of telling the story of the French River shooting did the fine work. The stranger who had dropped his pen and comb on French River was soon identified as one Norman Havre, alias "Black" McFay, alias Joe Hatte, known to the police. Louis Balenger's record was also known to them.

Chapter IX

THE SICK MAN

Jim McAllister and Noel fed Sherwood with milk, dosed him with quinine, bathed his hand with a hot solution of boric powder and touched it with iodine, placed hot compresses on his arm and bandaged him generously if not scientifically. He responded encouragingly to the treatment. It was easy to see that the pain in his arm had lessened. For a few hours of the afternoon he appeared to be cooler and felt cooler, lay awake without gabbling and slept without muttering and tossing. Once he recognized Noel Sabattis and spoke to him by name; and Noel patted his head and told him not to worry about anything for everything was going fine.

Sherwood was delirious during the night but not to the extent of the night before. In the morning he showed marked improvement, took his bitter dose of quinine as if he knew that it was good for him, drank an egg beaten up in milk, spoke affectionately to the red dogs and then to Jim McAllister, in puzzled tones, with something of recognition and more of fear and suspicion in his eyes.

"What are you going to do with me?" he asked.

"Take you home, Dick, and get a doctor for you," replied Jim.

"What's the idea?"

"I'm Jim McAllister. I live with my sister and young Ben O'Dell and your little girl—all one family—at O'Dell's Point. And that's where Noel and I mean to take you to. That's the idea. So there's nothing for you to worry about."

"Where's Louis Balenger?"

"You don't have to worry about him any more. He's dead."

"Yes, I remember that. Noel and I buried him. You remember that, Noel? He was dead, wasn't he?"

"Yep, he won't never move no more," replied the Maliseet.

"Did I shoot him?" asked the sick man.

"No, you didn't," said Jim sternly. "You weren't anywheres near him when he was shot; and if you hadn't been sickening with fever you wouldn't of run away. Balenger was shot by a man from Quebec and Ben O'Dell is hunting him this very minute."

"Who's Ben O'Dell?"

"He's John's son. Now you quit talking and take a rest."

"I was at John's funeral. You didn't know it but I was there. No one knew it, for I was ashamed to show myself. He was my friend. He was my company commander once."

"I know all about that, Dick. But you mustn't talk any more now. Yer a sick man."

Sherwood fell asleep. Jim and Noel made a stretcher of two poles, crosspieces and a pair of blankets; at ten o'clock they broke camp. They made a mile in slow time, then set the stretcher down and fed their patient. They marched again, walking with the utmost care, but Sherwood soon became excited and they had to halt, make a fire and bathe and dress his hand and arm. Again they dosed him and fed him. They rested until long past noon. They thought him to be asleep when they raised the stretcher for the third time, but he awoke instantly.

"Leave me alone!" he cried. "You can't fool me! I know you. You set a trap for me."

They kept on.

"That trap wasn't set for you, Dick," said McAllister over his shoulder. "That was a mistake."

"I didn't shoot Balenger, honest I didn't!" pleaded Sherwood. "I was going to—if I had the nerve—but I didn't do it. I was scared—afraid they'd hang me and Marion would starve—that's why I ran. But you set a trap for me—and caught me—and now you've got me."

"Nobody catch you!" cried Noel. "You all safe now. Jim an' me take you to Marion. You sick an' crazy, dat's all. Go to sleep. Shut up!"

He was quiet for a time but again broke out in terrified ravings before they had gone far. They had to set him down to quiet him. Again they built a fire, boiled the kettle, applied hot compresses to his arm. They fed him a hot drink and he went to sleep. But Jim saw that it would be dangerous to try to carry him farther that day, that all the traveling must be done in the morning when the fever was at its lowest. They had already covered about four of the eight miles. Old Noel rubbed his arms and said he had never before traveled such hard miles.

Jim was tired and anxious, but more anxious than tired. His anxiety was for the farm and his sister and the little girl almost as much as for the sick man. He was afraid of old Tim Hood, though he didn't admit it frankly even to himself. But Hood had always been a tricky character as well as a spiteful one and he had held a grudge against the O'Dells for many years; yesterday, when the old fellow's eyes had met his for an instant after the humiliating adventure with Red Chief, Jim had seen danger there. So after drinking a mug of tea he continued on his way, promising to return some time during the night. He took one of the rifles and Red Lily with him.

Jim reached home in time for supper. The last load of grain was in, but Bear and Sacobie and Mrs. Sacobie had not yet taken their departure. He asked all three to remain until after breakfast next morning, which they gladly agreed to do; and then, without his sister's knowledge, he arranged with the men that one should stand guard on the barns all night and one on the house. He told them that he had caught Tim Hood in the woods with a loaded rifle and disarmed him and that the old man was mad enough for anything. Hood was not popular with the Indians or any other poor and needy folk on the river, so Jim knew that the watch would be well kept.

He didn't say a word about Mel Lunt. He wasn't worrying about the constable, knowing that his worst faults were stupidity and professional vanity. That Lunt would try to get even with him was very likely, but by means and methods within the law—to the best of Mel's knowledge and belief, at least. He would probably make another effort to arrest Sherwood if he was able to obtain a warrant through the blundering of his superiors at Woodstock; and he was sure to try to get a warrant for Jim's arrest. But Jim didn't worry about anything Mel Lunt might do. Old Hood was the man he feared.

Jim managed a few minutes of private conversation with his sister, and they decided that if Sherwood should reach the house next day the little girl should be kept in ignorance of his identity—at least until medical care had cured him of his wild delirium. They believed that Doctor Scott and good nursing would accomplish this in a day or two. Little Marion was not of a prying disposition. To tell her that the sick man in the big spare room was not to be disturbed would be enough. The big spare room was so far from Mrs. O'Dell's room, in one corner of which Marion occupied a small bed, that there would be no danger of poor Sherwood's humiliating and pitiful and cruelly illuminating fever talk reaching the child's ears.

Jim spent a few minutes with the little girl before she went to bed. She took him to the library, set the lamp on the floor, sat down beside it and pulled a portfolio of old colored prints out from under one of the bookcases. She had discovered it a few days ago. The prints were of hunting scenes—of men in red coats and white breeches riding tall horses after red foxes, flying over green hedges, tumbling into blue brooks, but always streaming after the black and liver and white dogs who streamed after the fox.

"My dad once told me about that," said Marion. "He used to do it before he came out to this country, whenever he wasn't soldiering."

"Rough on the fox," said Uncle Jim. "Worse than trapping him, I guess. Why didn't they shoot him and be done with it?"

"That's what I said to dad," replied Marion. "But he said it wasn't so, for as soon as the fox felt tired he jumped into a hole in the ground and then the hunt was finished. They must have chased foxes a great many years in England, for I am sure these pictures are a great deal older than dad."

"Sure thing, much older," agreed Jim. "Those pictures were bought in London by Ben's great-grandfather."

The little girl returned the portfolio to its place and drew forth a shallow box of polished mahogany.

"Have you seen these, Uncle Jim?" she asked.

McAllister smiled. He had seen the contents of the box, but he also saw what she was up to. She was entertaining him in the hope that by so doing she might be allowed to sit up a few minutes past her usual bedtime.

"I don't mind seeing them again," he said.

She raised the lid of the box and disclosed to view two short brown pistols beautifully inlaid with silver about the grip and lock, a little metal flask, a cluster of bullets, a little ramrod, a lot of paper wads and dozens of tiny metal caps. All these curious articles lay on dark-green felt, the pistols in a central position, each of the different sorts of munitions in its own little compartment. The barrels of the pistols were short but large of bore.

"Ben showed me these," she said. "He told me all about how to load them. They are very, very old. You don't just put a cartridge in, like you do with a rifle or shotgun, but you ram the bullets and powder and wads down the muzzles, with that little stick and then put those little caps on, the same way Noel Sabattis does with his duck gun. I've seen Noel put the caps on his gun, but dad's was like a rifle. Noel's duck gun must be very old."

"Yes, but it's still of more use than those pistols ever were," replied Jim, thinking of the good work the Maliseet's great weapon had done

THEODORE G. ROBERTS

only yesterday and of the purpose for which the little dueling pistols had been so beautifully and carefully made in the ignorant days of the gay youth of one of Ben O'Dell's kind but conventional ancestors.

"What were the little pistols used for, Uncle Jim?" asked Marion.

"Well, you see, in the old days it wasn't all clover being a man of high family," he said. "It had its drawbacks. You were a man of mark, for sure. If a man is sassy to you nowadays, calls you names or anything like that, all you got to do is sass him back or kick him if you can; and all he can do is kick back—and that's all there is to it, no matter who you are or who yer grandfather used to be. But in the old days when these pistols were made it was different. If a man was rude to you then—said he didn't like the way yer nose stuck out of yer face or that the soldiers in yer regiment all had flat feet or maybe got real nasty and called you a liar—you had to throw a glassful of port wine or sherry wine into his face. Then it was up to him to ask you, as polite as pie, to fight a duel with him. And you had to do it or yer friends would say you weren't a gentleman—and that was considered a rough thing to say about a man in those days. So you had to do it, even if the law was against it. That's what those little pistols were for."

"To shoot gentlemen with?" asked the little girl in an awe-struck whisper.

"Yes—but they'd hit almost any kind of man if they were aimed right."

"And have these ones done that—shot people, Uncle Jim?"

"I guess they never shot anybody very seriously, dear. The O'Dell who owned them was a kind man, like all the O'Dells before and since, and brave as a lion and steady as a rock and a dead-sure shot. So whenever he was fussed and tricked into proving he was a gentleman— which everybody knew already—by fighting with a fool, he'd shoot the other lad in the hand that held the pistol—or the elbow or maybe the shoulder. It wasn't long before folks quit being rude to him."

Just then Mrs. O'Dell entered the library. Marion closed the box, shoved it back beneath the bookcase and kissed McAllister good night.

Jim posted Sol Bear and Gabe Sacobie, charged them to keep a sharp lookout and armed them with sled stakes. Enthusiastic Indians were not to be trusted with explosive weapons on such a job as this at night. And he left Red Lily with them. With two good Indians and a red dog outside and a squaw and another red dog in the kitchen he felt that old Tim Hood would not accomplish any very serious damage no matter how spiteful and reckless he might be feeling. Then he set out for the spot in the wilderness, due north and four miles away, where he had left the sick man and Noel Sabattis and Red Chief.

Jim might have spared himself these elaborate precautions had he known that Tim Hood's cowardice was still in excess of his rage. The old fellow still agreed with Mel Lunt, the thrice foiled but ever hopeful, that the safest and quickest way of getting in the first return blow at Jim McAllister was through the unfortunate Sherwood. So he continued to work with Lunt, to support the might and majesty of the law as interpreted by that persistent local constable. The O'Dell barns were not threatened that night. Sol and Gabe twirled their sled stakes in vain and at last fell asleep at their posts.

Jim found the camp without much difficulty. Sherwood was sleeping then but Noel said that he had been awake and raving for hours. Jim slept for an hour, then bathed and dressed the sick man's hand and arm, with Noel's assistance, dosed him with quinine and a full mug of cold water. All was quiet after that until about three o'clock, when Sherwood's restlessness again awoke the others. Again they applied hot compresses to his arm and gave him water to drink and tucked his blankets securely around him.

Sherwood awoke again shortly after dawn, hungry, clear of eye and as sane as you please. He drank fresh milk, a bottle of which Jim had brought in last night. He recognized Jim and of course he knew Noel Sabattis. He thanked them for all the trouble they were taking for him and said that he wasn't worth it.

"When I made sure Marion was safe and would soon be happy enough to forget me I didn't care how soon I pegged out," he said. "I was ill, very ill. The sickness had been in me for weeks, I think—I don't know how long. I was delirious even in the daytime and my nights were wide-awake nightmares. All my past haunted me. If I had ever been unkind to Julie or the baby I'd of gone mad and killed myself. But I'd never been unkind to them—not intentionally—just weak and a coward."

"You a'right now, anyhow," interrupted Noel. "Marion a'right too. Take annoder drink."

Sherwood drank obediently.

"The last night I crawled in," he continued, "and got my hand in that trap—well, that finished me! I don't know how I got the trap clear of my hand. I don't know how I got into the woods."

"My brother Ian set that trap and no one else knew anything about it," said Jim. "I guess he didn't stop to think what he was doing. Ben and I were away. But Doctor Scott'll fix yer hand, don't you worry."

"But will I be safe, Jim? From the law?"

"Sure thing! There's nothing you need fear the law about. I reckon Ben and Dave Brown know exactly who shot Balenger by this time and like enough they've caught him. But that don't matter one way or the other. The police know you didn't do it. But why didn't you tell us you wanted food? Why didn't you come right in and eat with us?"

"I was ashamed. And I was crazy with fear. I was sick, too—sick with fever, I suppose. I thought every one was hunting me to hang me and half the time I thought I'd really shot Balenger. I had a picture in my mind of just how I did it. But I couldn't go far away from the little girl."

"How was it the dogs never tackled you?" asked Jim.

"Never mind dat!" exclaimed Noel. "Shut up an' lay quiet! You shut up too, McAllister! You start him talkin' crazy ag'in, maybe."

"Dogs know me, and that red breed better than any," said Sherwood. "I think that the red dogs inherited a friendship for me."

"Maybe so, Dick; but Noel is right. Rest now. Don't try to think any more or yer fever'll be up again. We've got four miles to carry you yet."

They started after breakfast with Sherwood in the stretcher. They made the four miles by noon. They set the stretcher down behind a clump of bushes at the back of the barnyard and Jim went ahead to warn his sister and get little Marion out of the way. Marion was given lessons to learn in the library.

Sherwood was unconscious, murmuring, dry of hand and lip and flushed of brow by the time Jim laid him on the bed in the big spare room. His appearance shocked Mrs. O'Dell and at sight of his right hand she turned away to hide her tears. But she dried her tears and set to work as soon as the men had cut and pulled away Sherwood's tattered clothing and placed him between the cool sheets. She gave the torn hand and swollen arm the most thorough and tender treatment it had yet received.

The little girl was told of the sick man in the spare room whom Uncle Jim and Noel Sabattis had found in the woods. She was cautioned not to play in the hall outside his door or make a noise in the garden under his windows, for he was very weak and needed sleep. She was impressed. She questioned old Noel.

"Where did you find him in the woods, Noel?" she asked.

"Way off nort', layin' on de moss," replied Noel. "Red Chief find 'im first."

"Do you often find sick men lying in the woods?"

"Nope. Sometime."

"It is a good thing the bears didn't find him and eat him up."

"B'ars don't eat men up."

"I hope dad isn't in the woods still. I saw him go into the woods, away upriver, but he said he would come here for me in a few weeks."

"Sure, he come here for you. Come in two-t'ree days now, maybe."

"If he was sick and got lost in the woods like the man in the big spare room, what would happen to him, Noel?"

"What happen to him if he get lost in de woods, hey? Same what happen to dis feller—me an' Jim McAllister an' dese here dogs find 'im. Nobody git lost 'round here widout we find 'im quick an' fetch 'im home."

Jim drove away soon after dinner, headed for Woodstock and Doctor Scott. He reached the town in two hours. He drove to the doctor's house, only to learn that the doctor was out in the country, downriver, and wasn't expected home for an hour or two.

Jim stabled the mare, treated himself to a big cigar and strolled along Front Street. He was greeted by several people he knew. Soon he was greeted by a man he didn't know but who evidently knew him.

"Yer Jim McAllister, ain't you?" inquired the stranger, halting squarely in his path.

The stranger wore the uniform of a policeman. Jim didn't like his looks or his voice.

"Christened James," said Jim, dryly, "and with a handle in front of it when I'm smoking a fifteen-cent cigar."

"Yer wanted, Mister James McAllister," returned the other. "Come along, cigar an' all."

"Who wants me?"

"Sheriff Corker."

"Lead me to him, sonny. I can do some business with the sheriff myself. But I'm in a hurry."

They walked along side by side. The sheriff was not at home.

"We'll wait," said the policeman to the sheriff's cook.

Jim McAllister looked at his watch.

THEODORE G. ROBERTS

"I guess not," he said. "We'll call again, some other day."

"Guess again," returned the young man in blue.

"My second guess is the same," retorted Jim.

"I've heard about you, Mr. McAllister. Yer smart, but you ain't the only one. I know yer a game warden an' a big man upriver, but all that don't cut no ice to-day. There's a warrant out for you."

"You don't say! Sworn out by Mel Lunt and old Tim Hood, hey? Where is it, chief?"

"I ain't the chief. And I ain't got the warrant. But the sheriff will know what to do next."

"If he don't I can tell him. Mel got two, didn't he—two warrants? One was for Richard Sherwood, wasn't it?"

"That's right."

"Suppose we take a scout around for Sheriff Corker. I'm in a hurry."

"Guess we best set right here an' wait for him."

"What's yer name?"

"My name? Bill Simpson."

"Jerry Simpson's son, from down on Bent Brook."

"That's right, Mr. McAllister."

"I know yer father well. Smart man, Jerry Simpson. You look like him. Now about the hurry I'm in. There's a sick man out at the O'Dell house and I've got to get out to him with Doctor Scott. He's the man poor Mel Lunt's got the warrant out for. Mel's crazy. I've got Mel cold—and old Hood too—for toting rifles and ball ca'tridges through the woods in close season. There's nothing against Sherwood and Dave Brown is up in Quebec now, looking for the man who did the thing they're chasing poor Sherwood for. Mel Lunt is making a fool of Sheriff Corker. You come along with me, Bill, and save the sheriff's face—and maybe an innocent man's life, too. Mel's fool enough to drag Sherwood right out of bed, sick an' all."

"I'd sure like to do it, Mr. McAllister, but I dassint. I'm on duty in town all day. If I went with you I'd lose my job."

"Now that's too bad, but if you can't, you can't. The sheriff will wish you did when Dave Brown gets back from Quebec. I'll have to go by myself, then."

"Sorry, Mr. McAllister, but I got to keep you right here till the sheriff comes home. Rules is rules."

"And reason is reason, Bill—and when a man can't see reason it's time to operate on his eyes."

There was a brief, sharp scuffle in the sheriff's front hall. Young Bill Simpson proved too quick for Jim McAllister. He didn't hit any harder than he had to with his official baton—but it was too hard for Uncle Jim.

Chapter X

In the Nick of Time

By four o'clock, Richard Sherwood seemed to be as ill as when his friends had found him in the forest—as hot and dry with fever, as grievously tortured with pain, as blackly tormented of mind. That he was much stronger than he had been and that the mangled hand and inflamed arm looked better were just now the only indications of improvement.

Mrs. O'Dell and Noel Sabattis did everything they could think of for his relief. Mrs. O'Dell feared for his life, but old Noel was hopeful.

"Tough feller, Sherwood," he said. "Dat four-mile trip to-day fuss 'im up some, but he ain't so bad like when we find 'im. T'ink he dead man for sure dat time, me an' Jim. Doctor fix 'im a'right."

Mrs. O'Dell left the sick room for a little while. Marion saw tears on her cheeks.

"Won't the man from the woods get well, Aunt Flora?" she asked.

"He is very ill, dear—and in great pain—with a wounded hand," replied the woman, kissing her.

"Does Noel think he will have to be put in the ground—like Julie was—my mother Julie?"

The woman held the little girl tight for a moment.

"Noel thinks he will get well," she whispered.

At six o'clock Sherwood was sleeping quietly, heavy with fever and evidently unconscious of his hand. By seven he was tossing and talking wildly again. There was no sign of Jim McAllister or the doctor.

Eight o'clock came, and still there was no word or sign of Jim or Doctor Scott. The sick man was bathed in perspiration by this time.

"Dat fix 'em," said Noel to Flora O'Dell. "Dat sweat out de fever off his blood, a'right."

Marion went to bed at eight-thirty. Five minutes later wheels rumbled, the red dogs barked and a knock sounded on the kitchen door. Mrs. O'Dell heard the dogs and wheels and came hurrying down the back stairs. Noel, who was already in the kitchen, hastened to the door. The lamp was on the table behind him. He pulled the door wide open, and in the instant of recognizing Mel Lunt and old Hood on the threshold he also saw and recognized the muzzle of a shotgun within six inches of his chin.

Noel stepped back a few paces and the visitors followed him sharply. Hood kicked the door shut behind him just in time to keep out the red dogs. While Lunt kept Noel covered, Hood snapped the steel bracelets into place.

"Yer arrested," said Hood. "Where's McAllister?"

At that moment, both intruders saw Mrs. O'Dell standing near the foot of the back staircase, gazing at them with amazement and growing apprehension in her blue eyes.

"I don't want to p'int no weepon at a lady, but you come away from there an' set down an' keep quiet," said Lunt.

Mrs. O'Dell sat down on the nearest chair, which was only a few feet away from the narrow staircase.

"Where's yer brother Jim, ma'am?" asked Lunt.

"He went to Woodstock for a doctor," she replied.

"None o' yer lies, mind!" cried Hood.

The expression of Flora O'Dell's eyes changed, but she did not speak.

"Then he's in jail by this time," said Lunt.

"I don't understand," said Mrs. O'Dell, turning her darkling glance from Hood to Lunt. "He went to town for Doctor Scott. Why should he go to jail? And why have you put handcuffs on Noel Sabattis?"

"It be for us to ask questions an' for ye to answer 'em," cried old Hood in his worst manner. "Ye got a sick man here in the house, ain't ye? Come now, speak up sharp. Ain't no use yer lyin' to us."

"Yes, he is very sick," Mrs. O'Dell replied, her voice low and shaken. "He is dangerously ill. My brother has gone to get a doctor for him."

"He kin be doctored in jail," said Hood.

"That's right, ma'am," said Lunt. "The doctor can 'tend him in jail. We gotter take him now. Where is he?"

"It would kill him to move him to-night!"

"Well, what of it? He'll likely be hung anyhow," retorted the bitter old ferryman.

"That is not true and you know it!" cried Mrs. O'Dell. "You are persecuting him in wicked spite. You are a spiteful, hateful old man! And you, Melchar Lunt—you must be crazy to enter this house, armed, and threaten me and my guests!"

Hood uttered a jeering laugh.

"We got the warrants all straight and proper," said Lunt. "I'm in my rights, performin' my duty under the law, whatever ye may think. We wouldn't be so ha'sh if we wasn't in a hurry."

"You are in a hurry because you know that you haven't much time for your dirty, cruel, cowardly work, and you are afraid!"

"Misnamin' us won't help ye none, nor the murderer upstairs neither," sneered Hood, moving toward her.

She sprang to her feet and stood with her back to the narrow foot of the staircase. Noel Sabattis made a jump at Hood, but Lunt seized him and flung him down and threatened him with the gun. Hood advanced upon Mrs. O'Dell and suddenly clutched at her, grabbing her roughly by both arms. He gripped with all the strength of his short, hard fingers and tried to wrench her away from the staircase. She twisted, freed a hand and struck him in the face, twisted again, freed the other hand and struck him again. He staggered back with one eye closed, then rushed forward and struck furiously with his big fists, blind with rage and the sting in his right eye. Several blows reached her but again she sent him staggering back.

"Quit that!" cried Lunt. "Ye can't do that, ye old fool!"

He grabbed Hood by the collar, yanked him back and shook him.

"Are ye crazy?" he continued. "Young O'Dell would tear ye to bits for that! Go tie the Injun's legs. Then we'll move her out of the way both together, gentle an' proper, an' go git the prisoner."

Hood obeyed sullenly. He bound Noel's feet together with a piece of clothesline and tied him, seated on the floor, to a leg of the heavy kitchen table.

LITTLE MARION SHERWOOD HAD HEARD the dogs and the wheels and immediately slipped out of bed. Perhaps it was Ben, she had thought. That would be fine, for she missed Ben. Or it was Uncle Jim and the doctor from Woodstock to make the sick man well. She had gone to the top of the back stairs and stood there for a long time, listening, wondering at what she heard. She had been puzzled at first, then frightened, then angered. She had fled along the upper halls to the head of the front stairs and down the stairs. She had felt her way into the library and to a certain bookcase and from beneath the bookcase she had drawn the shallow, mahogany box which contained the little pistols with which gentlemen had proved themselves gentlemen in ancient days.

She had opened the box and worked with frantic haste—with more haste than speed. She had worked by the sense of touch alone and fumbled things and spilled things. Bullets had rolled on the floor, powder had spilled everywhere, wads and caps and the little ramrod had escaped from her fingers again and again; but she had retained enough powder, enough wads, two bullets and two caps. She had returned up the front stairs and along the narrow halls.

Now that Noel was tied down, Lunt stood his gun against the wall and gave all his attention to Mrs. O'Dell.

"I don't want to hurt ye," he said. "An' I ain't goin' to hurt ye. But I gotter go upstairs, me an' Tim Hood, an' fetch down the prisoner ye've got hid up there. I'm sorry Tim mussed ye up, ma'am, but ye hadn't ought to obstruct the law. Will ye kindly step aside, Mrs. O'Dell?"

"I won't! If you force your way past me and carry that man off to-night you'll be murderers, for he'll die on the road. If you try, I'll fight you from here every step of the way."

"We're in our rights, ma'am. I'm a constable an' here's the warrant. It ain't my fault he's sick—even if that's true. You grab her left arm, Tim, an' I'll take her right, an' we'll move her aside an' nip upstairs. But no rough stuff, Tim!"

A voice spoke in a whisper behind Mrs. O'Dell, from the darkness of the narrow staircase.

"Put your right hand back and take this pistol."

The woman recognized the voice but failed to grasp the meaning of the words. The little girl was frightened, naturally. That thought increased her unswerving hot rage against the men in front of her. She did not move or say a word in reply.

She felt something touch her right hand, which was gripped at her side. Again she heard the whisper.

"Take it, quick. It's all loaded, the way Ben told me. I have the other. Point it at them, quick!"

The men moved toward her. She opened her fingers and closed them on the butt of a pistol. She felt a weight on her shoulder and saw a thin arm and small hand and the other old dueling pistol extended past her ear. She raised her own right hand and cocked the hammer with a click.

"They are loaded!" cried the little girl shrilly. "And the caps are on, and everything. Ben showed me how to load them. And I'll pull the trigger if you come another step, you old man with the queer whiskers! The bullets are big. And I put two in each pistol and plenty of powder."

"Stand close together, you two, and move to the left," said Mrs. O'Dell. "Do you hear me, Lunt? Do as I tell you, or I'll shoot—and so will the little girl. These are real pistols. That's right. That's far enough. Stand there and stand steady."

"This is a serious matter, Mrs. O'Dell," exclaimed Lunt. "You are guilty of threatenin' the law with deadly weapons—of resistin' it with firearms."

Mrs. O'Dell put up her left hand and relieved the child of the other pistol, at the same time speaking a few words in a low voice but without taking her glance or her aim off the intruders. Marion slipped past her, ran over and took Lunt's gun from where he had stood it against the wall.

"Steady, both of you," warned the woman. "Keep your eyes on me. You will notice that I am not aiming at your heads. I'm aiming at your stomachs—large targets for so short a range."

Marion carried the shotgun over to the table and placed it on the floor beside old Noel Sabattis. Then, moving swiftly and with precision, she opened a drawer in the table, drew out a knife and cut the thin rope which bound the Maliseet's legs together and to the table.

Noel seized the gun at the breech with his manacled hands and got quickly to his feet. With both hands close together on the grip of the stock, he pushed the lever aside with a thumb. The breech fell open, disclosing the metal base of a cartridge. He closed the breech by knocking the muzzle smartly on the edge of the table. His hands had only an inch of play, but that was enough. They overlapped around the slender grip, with the hammer within easy reach of a thumb and the trigger in the crook of a finger.

"Dat a'right," he said, glancing over the intruders. "Good gun, hey? Light on de trigger, hey?"

"Sure she's light on the trigger!" cried Lunt. "Mind what ye're about, Noel! A joke's a joke—but ye'll hang for this if ye ain't careful!"

Noel smiled and told them to sit down on the floor. They obeyed reluctantly, protesting with oaths. Then he asked the little girl to open the door and admit the dogs, which she did. The red dogs bounded into the kitchen, took in the situation at a glance and surrounded the two seated on the floor. Red Chief and Red Lily showed their gleaming fangs, whereupon old Tim Hood became as silent and still as a man of wood.

"I think you have them safe, Noel," said Mrs. O'Dell.

Noel nodded.

"Then I'll go up and give him his quinine," she said, handing the pistols over to the enthusiastic little girl.

Noel and Marion sat down on chairs in front of the constable and the ferryman. The three dogs stood. Everything pointed at the two on the floor—five pairs of eyes, the muzzles of firearms and the muzzles of dogs.

"Forgit it, Noel," said Mr. Lunt. "Cut it out. What's the use? I'm willin' to let bygones be bygones. Call off yer dogs an' swing that there gun o' mine off a p'int or two an' Tim an' me will clear out. Careful with them pistols, little girl, for Heaven's sake! Noel, ain't she too young to be handlin' pistols? She might shoot herself."

Noel smiled and so did Marion.

"I'll give ye the warrants, Noel, an' say no more about it," continued the constable. "We got three warrants here—an' the charges agin' ye are real serious—but I'm willin' to forgit it. So there ain't no sense in keepin' us here, clutterin' up Mrs. O'Dell's kitchen."

"She don't care," replied Noel. "An' Marion don't care. You like it fine, Marion, hey? 'Taint every night you git a chance for to set up so late like dis, hey?"

"Yes, thank you, I enjoy it," said the little girl. "It is great fun. It is like a story in a book, isn't it, Noel?"

"Hell!" snorted old Tim Hood.

Noel cocked an eye at the ferryman and he cocked the gun at the same time.

"Lemme unlock yer handcuffs for ye," offered Lunt. "Ye'll feel more comfortable without 'em, Noel."

"Guess not," returned Noel. "Feel plenty comfortable a'ready."

Wheels sounded outside, and voices; and the youngest of the red dogs barked and turned tail to his duty and frisked to the door. The others stood firm and kept their teeth bared at the men on the floor, but their plumed tails began to wag. Old Noel's glance did not waver, but Marion's eyes turned toward the door.

The door opened and men crowded into the kitchen and halted in a bunch and stared at the unusual scene before them. There was Doctor Scott, with a black bag in his hand. There was Uncle Jim, with a white bandage on his head which made his hat too small for him. And there was Sheriff Corker fixing a cold glare on the two men seated on the floor. And over all showed the smiling face of young Ben O'Dell.

Jim McAllister was the first to speak.

"Where's Flora?" he asked.

"Upstairs," answered Noel. "Everyt'ing a'right an' waitin' for de doctor."

He stood up, lowered the hammer of the gun and placed the weapon on the table.

"Now you take dis handcuffs off darn quick, Mel Lunt," he said.

The constable scrambled heavily to his feet and obeyed.

Doctor Scott crossed the room and vanished up the narrow stairs. Sheriff Corker found his voice then and addressed Lunt and old Tim Hood at considerable length and with both force and eloquence. His words and gestures seemed to make a deep and painful impression on them, but the rest of the company paid no attention. Ben kissed the little girl, shook hands with Noel Sabattis, grabbed the leaping dogs in his arms, told fragments of his Quebec adventures to any one who chose to listen and asked question after question without waiting for the answers.

Uncle Jim seated himself beside the table and lit a cigar, cool as a cucumber, smiling around. Sheriff Corker marched Lunt and Hood out of the kitchen and out of the woodshed, still talking, still gesticulating violently with both hands. Those in the kitchen heard wheels start and recede a minute later. Marion went to Uncle Jim and asked him what he had done to his head. He told her of his difficulty with the young policeman which had caused all the delay, of the home-coming of the sheriff when Doctor Scott was bandaging his head, and of the arrival of Ben and Mr. Brown at the sheriff's house a few minutes later.

"But what are you doing with those old pistols?" he asked.

"Those two men came to take the sick man away," she said. "They tied Noel to the table and fought with Aunt Flora. I heard them; so I loaded the pistols—and then they were at our mercy."

Mrs. O'Dell appeared and ran into her son's arms. She backed out presently, and they both moved over to where Uncle Jim and the little Sherwood girl sat side by side, hand in hand. Noel Sabattis and the dogs followed them.

"The doctor says it is slow fever, but that the worst is over with," said Mrs. O'Dell. "He must have had it for weeks and weeks. And the arm can be saved. The crisis of the fever came to-night—and a drive into town to-night would have killed him." She slid an arm around the little girl. "But for Marion, they would have taken him," she continued. "Noel was tied to the table and I couldn't have kept them off much longer—and she loaded the dueling pistols in the dark and brought them to me—just in the nick of time."

"She saved his life, sure enough," said Jim McAllister.

"Flora done mighty good too," spoke up old Noel Sabattis. "She fit 'em off two-t'ree time an' bung Hood on de eye."

Mrs. O'Dell laughed and blushed.

"I did my best—but you and the old pistols saved him, dear," she whispered in Marion's ear. "And by to-morrow, perhaps, or next day, he will be well enough to thank you."

The child looked intently into the woman's eyes and the lights in her own eyes changed gradually. Her thin shoulders trembled.

"Who—is—he?" she whispered in a shaken thread of voice.

"Your very own dad," replied Mrs. O'Dell, kissing her.

Jim McAllister made coffee. The doctor joined the men in the kitchen, for his patient was sleeping. Ben told of his and Mr. Brown's successful search for the man who had shot Louis Balenger on French River. He admitted that the actual capture of Balenger's old enemy had been made by the police of Quebec—but he and Dave had been very busy. While he talked he toyed with the pistols which Marion had left on the table. He removed the caps. He looked into one barrel and saw that it was loaded to within a fraction of an inch of the muzzle. He produced a tool box in the shape of a knife from his pocket and opened a blade that looked like a small ice pick. With this he picked a few paper wads out of the barrel. With the last wad came a stream of black powder.

"Hullo!" he exclaimed, forgetting his adventures in Quebec.

He thumped the muzzle of the pistol on the table until another wad came out, followed by two bullets. The others, watching intently, exchanged glances in silence. Ben withdrew the charge from the other pistol.

"She put the bullets in first!—in both of them!" he cried.

"But it worked," said Uncle Jim. "It turned the trick. She saved her pa's life—so I guess *that's* all right!"

THE END

A Note About the Author

Theodore G. Roberts (1877–1953) was a Canadian novelist and poet, soldier, and journalist. Born into a literary family, he had his first poetry published when he was only twelve. As a journalist he was sent to Cuba to cover the Spanish-American War and developed malaria, which would trouble him for the rest of his life. He was a world traveler and served with the British army in the First World War. His travel and military service informed his writings, but his more than thirty books of adventure stories and poetry display most often a direct and vital connection to the landscape and people of his beloved native Canada.

A Note from the Publisher

Spanning many genres, from non-fiction essays to literature classics to children's books and lyric poetry, Mint Edition books showcase the master works of our time in a modern new package. The text is freshly typeset, is clean and easy to read, and features a new note about the author in each volume. Many books also include exclusive new introductory material. Every book boasts a striking new cover, which makes it as appropriate for collecting as it is for gift giving. Mint Edition books are only printed when a reader orders them, so natural resources are not wasted. We're proud that our books are never manufactured in excess and exist only in the exact quantity they need to be read and enjoyed.

Discover more of your favorite classics with Bookfinity™.

- Track your reading with custom book lists.
- Get great book recommendations for your personalized Reader Type.
- Add reviews for your favorite books.
- AND MUCH MORE!

Visit **bookfinity.com** and take the fun Reader Type quiz to get started.

Enjoy our classic and modern companion pairings!